The Pretty Diva Story

Rocko Dupas

First Mass Market Printing January 2023

First Trade Paperback Printing January 2023

Edit by : Rocko Dupas and Antoine Jolivette

ISBN:9798367426830

DEDICATION

This book is dedicated to all the Pretty Divas around the world. Please remember it does not matter your race, creed, nationality or your beautiful look, there's a little diva in all of you. This book is also dedicated to The Dupas Family and a special diva, Symone. Life sometimes takes us down paths we didn't intend to go down. But we have to get up and keep on trying. I hope you see me in this new form. And, may God bless all of y'all.

TABLE OF CONTENTS

ACKNOWLEDGMENTS

First and foremost, if you have made it this far, I want to give a very special thanks to you. This is my first book and I hope my writing did not disappoint. The Pretty Diva Story is about freedom, love, greed, loyalty, jealousy, and envy, which are the things we deal with in out everyday lives. Thanks to all the wonderful writers I've befriended over the past year, especially Just Rick (Richard Spraggins). To Antoine and Shelton Jolivette, Avery Goodstory, Curt Vice, Anthony Thompson, Gerry Chaney, Brandon Walker and MBridges. You all gave me examples to follow and taught me how to think outside the box. Because of y'all, I look at life differently. Thanks for helping me become a good writer and an even better man. I wanted this story to be different from most and you all help me craft it and accomplish just that. Once again, thanks for everything. To Delilah, Deena Sanchez, Breonna, Alejandra, Rosa, Rosanna, Diamond, Ashley Sanchez, and Jazmin. Thanks for being strong independent women. And, to the most prettiest diva in the world, I'll like to apologize for not being better. But, Daddy will always love you no matter what anyone says. I love you, Makayla. Special thanks to everyone who told me to keep pushing and to finish the book. There is no big secret that we live in a challenging time. But, truly family and friends are the ones who help us make it through. My aunt Yolanda told me to keep my head up because with every hardship comes ease. Now, I know what she meant. Finally, I would like to thank those who said I wouldn't make it and had no interest in helping me through my trials and tribulations. I truly wouldn't be here if it wasn't for you. I love you all. The trilogy has just begun so please look out for more writings by Rocko Dupas. If I missed you, please know it was not on purpose!

A Diva is the female version of a Hustler

— Beyoncé Knowles

CHAPTER 1 - DREAMZ

Years in foster care didn't stop Ronisha Beaudruex from believing her dreams would never come true. Growing up in Houston, Texas, bouncing around from one state home to the next, struggling to fit in, she refused to lose hope. Ronisha Beaudruex knew one day she would be somebody and not just another "product of the system."

In high school, not only was she voted most likely to succeed, she had graduated at the top of her class. Her peers noted her intelligence and beauty by voting her prom queen. Her tough skin developed from years in foster care and her determination knew no limits. Pell grants and part-time jobs paid for her college. It led to a job as a financial advisor for a local bank. But she wanted more, and she never stopped dreaming.

One night while in bed, she thought about her older brother, Cory. Cory was shot last year. A mystery never solved. She loved and missed him. She respected him just like everyone else even though they knew he sold drugs. But Cory gave back. Cory loved his community and enjoyed helping people who were less fortunate. Ronisha didn't judge her brother. How could she? He provided for his family. Besides, she occasionally smoked marijuana herself. She fell asleep wondering if she could ever sell drugs like Cory had.

In the morning she decided. The business her brother left behind could be hers. An operation she could not only run, but grow. She would make it bigger, better and she would make more money than her bank job could provide.

Weeks passed before she bumped into a runner that ran for Cory's business. The young man informed her the operation had been taken over by Ramon. Ramon and Cory had met selling nickels and dimes. Ramon had shown him how to grow his own weed and Cory turned it into an empire. He also told her Ramon had left on business in California. He co-owned a dispensary with his sister and if she wanted to meet with him, she would have to wait until he returned. She asked the runner to make the call to set up everything. Ramon agreed to the meeting.

Days later, Ronisha called her friend Vonshee. "Are you coming with me?" she asked her friend, Vonshee.

"You're really serious about this, Nisha?"

"I'm dead serious."

"Really?"

"Yes. You, Bree and I are going to take over that business."

"You want Bree in on this? You know how she gets with money and men."

"Yeah, but she could bring in a lot of business. Especially from all the ballers she meets at the club she dances at."

"Well, she's been acting like Bonnie and Clyde ever since she met that Jeremy guy."

Nisha laughed. "I know, what does she call him again?"

"She calls him, J-Dub."

"Anyways, be ready at two. I'll pick you up then."

After ending the call, Ronisha glanced in the mirror. Amazed at how her Chanel dress wrapped around her 32D-25-40 frame. She stood five foot five and weighed one hundred and forty pounds and her dress showed every curve on her body and she couldn't complain.

About an hour and a half later, Nisha and Vonshee drove to Ramon's mini mansion in Sugarland, Texas outside of Houston. The five bedroom, three and a half bathroom with a four car garage was amazing.

"This house looks like it belongs in a Dupont Magazine," Vonshee said.

Ronisha had always known her brother's operation brought in money. But if his right hand man lived like this, she was one hundred percent sure she wanted in.

After parking, they were met by a man who introduced himself as Charles. He escorted them into the living room.

Moments later, Ramon walked in with his hands spread wide."Ladies, welcome to Ramon's Casa." Doing a double take at Ronisha's beauty, he seemed struck by her beautiful long curly hair that ran down her back and her curves that made his eyes follow down, stopping at her hips. After a pause, he shot his eyes back to the women and offered his hand.

"Ramon, but my friends call me Maine, pronounced like the state."

Ronisha laughed. "Ronisha, but my friends call me Nisha. And, this beautiful woman to my right is my bestie, Vonshee."

"Nice to meet you both," Ramon said, shaking their hands. "Ms. Nisha, has anyone ever told you that you look like someone famous?"

Nisha giggled. "Yup, they say I look just like Beyonce."

Vonshee laughed. "Girl stop."

Ramon chuckled. "Well, what can I do for you ladies today?"

Nisha whistled. "I heard you were running my brother's operation now?"

Ramon smiled. "We ran this operation together. I showed him how to grow. Cory showed me how to be a better businessman. The operation had been helping so many people so I didn't want to just shut it down after Cory's passing."

"I'm glad you kept it running, but we want in on my brother's business." Nisha said.

"And, being family it's only right," Vonshee added.

Shocked by the words that left Nisha's lips. "Who are we? Is that french?" Ramon asked.

"My crew, me, Vonshee, and my homegirl, Bree."

"I can't just bring you in on something he and I built over years just because you're his sister."

"I'm not asking for his damn operation. I just want in."

Ramon studied them for a moment. Putting his hands up in a surrendering motion, he said, "How about this? I'll front you and your crew some pounds, teach you about the operation. Then you can run your own operation. But there's one catch."

"What's the catch?" Vonshee asked.

"Y'all keep me as your supplier."

Nisha's smile crept to her face.

"We can do that."

"Deal," Ramon said. "Now where's this Bree at?"

"She couldn't be with us today. She had to do something with her baller boyfriend, J-Dub."

Ramon laughed. "Did you just say J-Dub?"

"Yes, do you know him?" Nisha asked.

"Well yeah, Cory brung him in after he got back from the army. He knew him from high school. Damn, it's a small world, huh?"

"I guess," Nisha replied.

"Back to the topic. I'm only doing this because Cory was like my little brother. So, we're practically like family," Ramon said.

Nisha smiled seductively. "No, we're not."

As Ramon spoke, a few words went in one ear and out of Nisha's other. Ramon was well dressed, handsome, clean cut, and had an athletic build. He was even probably good in bed. Coming back to earth, Nisha's eyes were glued to him.

Ramon cleared his throat. "Hello?"

"Huh," Nisha answered.

He smiled, knowing he had her in a trance. "If you really want this. I'll call you when we set everything up."

Nisha turned to Vonshee. "What do you think?"

"That's fine with us," Vonshee replied.

"Great, I'll call with information on where to meet us and I'll show you everything you need to know about the operation. Then we'll see if you and your crew will still be willing to be down with this lifestyle."

Nisha looked around the mansion. "Oh, trust me, we're down."

"Since we're all friends now, can we call you Maine?" Vonshee asked.

Ramon laughed. "Naw, I prefer you call me Ramon. We're family now."

Hours after talking, Ramon walked both ladies to their car. He opened both doors for them and as he closed Nisha's door, she caught him staring at her body and she loved it. "It was nice meeting you, Mr. Ramon."

"It was my pleasure."

"So, we'll be expecting a call from you?" Nisha asked, smiling.

"Yes, I'll most definitely be calling you, Ms. Nisha."

"And, I'll most definitely be waiting."

Nisha drove away and watched Ramon stare until she made a right off the street.

"You like him don't you?" Vonshee asked Nisha.

"This isn't the time to be liking anyone," Nisha grinned.

"Okay, whatever, I think his runner Charles is cute."

Nisha laughed. "Girl stop. Now call Bree and tell her what's up."

Vonshee reached into her Gucci purse, pulled out her phone and called Bree on speaker phone.

"Bree speaking, now it's your turn."

"Nisha and I just left Ramon's crib and we're in there."

"Are y'all serious?"

"Dead serious," Nisha said from the driver's seat.

After dropping Vonshee off, Nisha cruised Houston. Riding around she had thought about a better life and she knew it was out there. That's why she studied twice as hard as her classmates. She became a nerd at Westbury High School. But her beauty and curves is what made her popular. She became friends with Vonshee, Bree, and an army brat named Simerrah who left the states when her father was called back to duty overseas.

For two weeks, Nisha waited on Ramon's phone call. She had almost given up when he finally called.

"Meet me at 6309 West Bellfort at five o'clock sharp and dress in your most professional attire."

Ramon hung up before Nisha could reply. She glanced at her Apple Watch and she had three hours for her and her crew to meet Ramon. She called Bree and Vonshee. Nisha wanted to explain their next move.

After pulling into the home's driveway, Nisha took notice of the place. It was in a not so bad neighborhood. The grass was neatly trimmed and two pit-bulls were running around the front yard. Nisha always loved dogs, she petted them after exiting the car. While rubbing the male dog, she read his name tag.

"Little Cory. I wonder what her name is," she said as she grabbed the female's name tag and read, "London, Property of Ramon."

One of Ramon's runners led them inside. The house was beautiful. Mosaic tiled floors, green marble counters, flat screens everywhere and a mini bar. Not your average drug dealer's pad.

"Welcome ladies to grow house number one," Ramon said, entering the room.

The ladies admired the house as Ramon requested they follow him to a back room. All of his workers were there including J-Dub. J-Dub's eyes followed his girlfriend, Bree as she walked by with the group.

"This room here is the germ room. This is where we germinate all of the seeds, mother them, and care for them until they're ready for the next stage."

"What's the next stage?" Nisha asked.

"Once the plants reach their leaf stage, we move them to the next room where we give them a nice source of light and water every twelve hours. When they're fully budded or flowered, then we harvest them. We clip them, hang them, dry them out and then we go and package them. Sometimes we might even clone a plant.

"For real?" Vonshee asked, amazed.

"Yup," Ramon answered. "We do different methods for different plants. It really just depends on the growers and the plants."

"Which ones will we be selling?" Bree asked.

"Well we have different types here. You can pick which one you want to sell later."

"So, what type of weed do you grow here?" Nisha asked curiously.

Ramon's eyes widened and he grinned. "We have here at this establishment King Louie, Green Crack, White Widow, Chem Dawg, Bruce Banner, Purple Haze, and our number one seller, OG Kush. I'm also creating my own. But I haven't gave it a name yet."

"Wow!" Nisha said.

"So, how much do you make?" Vonshee asked.

"Well each plant produces four ounces every three months-"

"Yeah, but how much do you make?" Bree asked, cutting Ramon off.

Ramon sighed and rolled his eyes. "Every four plants equals a pound. We have over 800 plants in each house. That's 1,600 times the average price of $2,000 a pound. So, we make around $3,200,000 a year."

"Are you fucking serious? You make that much selling weed?" Nisha asked, scratching her head.

"Sometimes more," Ramon replied. "I also got a pill connect."

The women stared at each other amazed and wide eyed.

"Any other questions?" Ramon asked.

As the women looked at each other and shrugged. Ramon asked Charles to bring in a fresh batch. When Charles returned, Ramon asked, "Does anyone want to test the product?"

All three women raised their hands high.

After the smoke session, Vonshee asked, "So when do we get this?"

"That depends on your boss, Nisha. After I train her, she'll train you two and you'll go from there," Ramon answered.

Blowing smoke from her nose. "I got us baby girl," Nisha said in a smooth low tone.

Minutes later, Nisha and her crew left. She took both women home and then decided to call it an early night, still feeling good from the marijuana high.

CHAPTER 2 – TRAINING DAY

For several weeks, Ramon gave knowledge and information about the operation. He even told Nisha about the corruption of cops and people who might envy her sudden appearance. She impressed him on how rapidly she understood everything. He told her Cory always said she was a smart young woman. But, what he didn't know, she had an IQ of 153, she was basically a genius. Throughout the whole training, Nisha came up with different ways and schemes on how to make money faster and less riskier. Nisha advanced so far in the information she received, she began to train her crew before her training was done. When Ramon finished with her training, she requested another meeting to discuss numbers.

"So, Mr. Ramon, how much are you willing to front me and my crew on our first run?" Nisha asked.

Pausing a moment, he finally said, "I'll front you and your crew ten pounds of the good stuff."

Nisha smiled. "We can handle ten."

"I bet you can," Ramon replied.

While Ramon talked, Nisha calculated numbers in her head and realized if she sold each gram at $15 her profit would be $420 an ounce. If she charged $10 the profits would be $280 an ounce. Each pound would profit over $4,000 depending how and who she sold to. Her thinking was suddenly stopped when she heard Bree ask a question.

"What's your cut, Ramon?"

"Yeah, what is your cut?" Nisha asked. "How much do you want?"

"Well, my first cut is always 250. After that, we'll discuss a different number," Ramon answered.

When the women left, Nisha asked them where they wanted to eat. Everyone in sync agreed on The Cheesecake Factory. After arriving, Nisha told them to and get seats while she made a call. She called Cory's wife Karla to check on her and the twins. Karla's voice mail picked up. Nisha didn't want to leave a voicemail. She believed voice mails could get you in trouble in the future.

After the call, Nisha walked into the scratch kitchen restaurant and was greeted by a hostess with beautifully applied make-up, long black hair, and slightly exposed breast with curves that were out of this world. Making eye contact, Nisha couldn't look away.

"Hello, I'm Selena, Welcome to The Cheesecake Factory," the spicy looking Latina said.

"Hi," Nisha began, "I'm looking for my friends, they came in here a few minutes ago."

"Oh, yes ma'am, you must be Ms. Beaudruex. Follow me and I'll take you to them. They said you were right behind them."

"Well, lead the way, *Mamacita*."

Following the Latina, Nisha whispered, "Damn, she's fine as hell." She watched the hostess' hips swing from left to right in a hypnotizing motion.

"Here they are," Selena said, smiling and extending her arm.

"Thanks boo," Nisha said, smiling in return.

"*No problema*, enjoy your meal."

"We've already ordered three Mojitos," Vonshee said.

"And, your favorite, Factory Nachos."

"Great, while we wait, let's discuss business. I've put together a plan for our operation," Nisha said, sliding into her seat next to Bree.

"Well, give It to us," Bree said, giving Nisha space.

"Okay Bree, since you work at D-Live, you can sell to all the ballers and dancers who like to spend money. Vonshee, since you work at the smoke shop, you can sell to the smokers. But, only to the ones who come in and spends the most money."

"Then, what will you do? Vonshee asked, squinting at Nisha.

The waitress dropped off their drinks before Nisha answered. Nisha took a sip of her mojito and said, "I'll sell to some old connects from college and the bank."

A minute later the appetizer arrived, Nisha grabbed a chip, dipped it into cheese and said, "Give me time and I promise we'll be millionaires running the city."

The waitress returned and the women made their orders. Nisha ordered her usual, the Jambalaya Pasta with extra sausages. Vonshee ordered the Chicken Alfredo Pasta and Bree ordered the Southern Fried Catfish. The waitress double checked the orders and left.

"Can I ask you a question, Nisha?" Bree asked.

"Sure."

"How did you and Cory end up in foster care?"

"Well," Nisha said, "When I was seven years old my mom and dad got into a big custody battle. Cory and I ended up in C.P.S. While in foster care my dad signed over his rights to the state. My mom went to jail for selling drugs to an undercover. Texas took her parental rights. So, Cory and I got lost in the system. We finally reached somewhere stable and stayed there. My foster mom passed away right after I graduated."

"You never tried to find her?" Vonshee asked, biting her lower lip.

"Once, then I realized if she wanted us she would have surely found us. Cory felt the same way. We just stuck together and looked after each other."

"Wow," Bree said.

"I do remember her selling drugs when we were young. I guess that's a skill she past on to Cory. And, me too," Nisha said, smirking.

"Well, we're your family now," Bree said, putting her arms around Nisha.

"Thanks. And speaking of family. I called Karla to check on the twins but she didn't answer. I guess I'll call her later."

After enjoying their meals, they ordered three strawberry cheesecakes to go. They tipped the waitress nicely and before leaving, Nisha was stopped by Selena.

"I'm sorry to bother you but, I think you are so beautiful," Selena said.

Nisha blushed. "Thanks, I do get that sometimes."

"I was wondering if it's not a problem. Can I have your number?"

Shocked and intrigued, Nisha asked, "You want my number?"

"Yes, if it's okay," Selena said, smiling.

"Sure, I'll give you my number. But, you have to give me yours."

"Sure," Selena said, passing Nisha a paper with her number on it and her phone.

Nisha grabbed both and programmed her number into Selena's phone. "Call me," Nisha said, handing Selena back her phone.

After they exchanged numbers, Nisha turned away and walked to her car.

Vonshee and Bree were standing, waiting, and smiling.

"Did she just ask for your number?" Bree asked.

Nisha blushed.

"I think she has a crush on you," Vonshee laughed.

"You both need to quit. Now, get in so we can leave," Nisha said, as they all entered the car.

Nisha dropped off her friends and told them to be ready that weekend.

Ramon had told her that their pounds would be delivered next Friday. Nisha headed home. She hated going home to an empty house. Her last relationship went south after her ex-boyfriends Brocko went to jail for three years. When Brocko was released from a Texas prison, he found her and they dated again. But the relationship wasn't the same. They both had grown into two different people during their separation. Then she dated a low level drug dealer by the name of Quincy. But, that relationship didn't last long. Quincy had gotten into an altercation with a police officer and was charged with Aggravated Assault on a Public

Servant. The Judge sentenced him to serve eight years. Nisha did her part as a girlfriend with an incarcerated boyfriend. But, Quincy still would treat her badly, accusing her of cheating when she couldn't answer his calls. After all the drama, she never answered another call and hasn't taken any relationship seriously since. She truly enjoyed the single life, but she also missed being someone's better half.

CHAPTER 3 – MAJOR MOVES

Friday came in a breeze. Nisha woke up, bathed, brushed her teeth, applied her make-up, and got dressed. After receiving the front from Ramon, she started making moves. Throughout the next week, she contacted multiple people and told them she was selling. The first week she moved a pound by herself and made $4,000. She and her crew was doing better than she expected and her phone was ringing off the hook. She loved it and she had became addicted to the money transactions.

Looking at the clock on her radio, she picked up her phone and called Bree. Bree answered, doing her signature pick up that everyone knew her for. "Bree speaking, now it's your turn."

Nisha chuckled. "What are you doing, Bree?"

"Just getting up?"

"Well, get your ass up. You know money don't sleep."

"Do you know what type of night I just had?"

"I don't even want to know," Nisha answered. "Did you make some moves?"

"Yes," Bree said, yawning. "I got this guy's number and he said he wants to buy a pound every week. He sounds like a small-time hustler. But I think he's legit. And I think I've moved about three quarters of a pound so far."

"Good, now I need to call Vonshee and check up on her. Girl's Night later, so you better be there."

"Okay, but let me get some more sleep."

Nisha laughed. "Girl, you ain't that tired. I'll call you later."

After ending the call, Nisha dialed Vonshee's number.

"Hello sexy," Vonshee answered, laughing.

"What are you doing, sexy?" Nisha giggled.

"Well, if you must know, Boss Lady. I'm at the smoke shop. That shit Ramon gave us something that sells like McDonald's Hot Cakes."

"Well, it is some good weed."

"How would you know?" Vonshee curiously asked.

"I had to test the product."

"Yeah, okay," Vonshee replied.

"I only sold exclusive customers some, well people I considered exclusive."

"That's good, baby girl. Everything is lining up."

"Yes, and they keep returning like it's crack or something."

Nisha laughed. "They're supposed to and I have to call you back. I have a customer calling me."

*****

On the other side of town, Ramon was getting ready for his day. He usually woke up in his king size bed. Today was no different. After taking care of his morning business he made himself a cup of coffee. He planned out his day as he always did. He walked into his four car garage, looked at his cars and opted to drive his red and black Challenger Hellcat. Everyone loved it just as much as he did. J-Dub loved it so much he bought an identical one. But, it lacked his performance package. Ramon's first stop was to grow house number one. He and Cory picked the house out themselves. They chose the neighborhood to avoid the stereos-type of a normal drug dealer making his money out of a run down trap house.

Ramon arrived at the first grow house and met J-Dub in the driveway.

"What's good, Maine?" J-Dub asked.

"Same like everyday. Trying to take over the world."

"Have you considered the new coke connect I hooked you up with?"

Ramon shrugged his shoulders. "Look, the few coke runs we did were good, but I don't think I want my crew really associating with that coke shit."

"What the fuck? Are you serious!?" J-Dub yelled.

Lifting his head from his phone, Ramon calmly asked, "Who the fuck are you yelling at?"

"I'm just saying. I already told my connect Facts that we going to buy some more from him."

"Well, tell him I changed my mind."

J-Dub stared Ramon down for a couple of seconds, then he walked off with disappointment on his face.

"What is it with coke and this guy?" Ramon asked himself, walking toward the front door.

Ramon walked through the door and saw everything was running smoothly. He and his crew were making money, more money than they had made in the past years. He never worried about undercover law enforcements or even envious people who wanted his throne. It felt good to be on top. But he also felt lonely.

And the business didn't feel right without his best friend. He envied Cory a little. Cory had became a known drug dealer, but he had a family, a wife to go home to, and two kids he truly loved. Ramon respected that Cory had always put his family first before his business. Ramon wanted to leave the streets and start a family also. But he couldn't leave his crew behind. Not before finding out what happened to Cory. His ringing cell phone caused him to snap back to reality. He looked down and saw it was Nisha.

"Hello," he answered smoothly, calmly, and collectively.

"Well, look who came out to play." Nisha giggled through the ear piece.

"Well, you know business first. Then, playing comes next."

"That's true. That's why I'm out here making moves."

"So you're officially a dope girl now?"

"You can say that," Nisha said with sarcasm. "Vonshee and I are going to D-Live tonight. Bree dances there. I want to invite you to join us."

Ramon paused. "I suppose I could slide by."

"Good, it was supposed to be girls night but I changed my mind. And, bring Charles. Vonshee likes him for some reason," Nisha laughed.

"I can do that. What time do you want to meet up?"

"Around eleven, and don't be late."

"What kind of boss would I be if I showed up to a meeting late."

After conversing, they hung up. Ramon drove to the second grow house. He parked his Hellcat and proceeded toward the front door. A young woman named Lori opened it.

"Hey Fantasia,"

"Lori," Lori said, smiling.

"Well, you know you look like Fantasia so that's what I'm gonna keep calling you."

"Yes, I know I look like her, but what are you doing here?"

"Just making my daily rounds?"

"Well, everything is going well. I'm pretty sure you can smell it. I want to invest into some new ventilators. The old ones still work, but we could always upgrade," Fantasia said, holding her high tech tablet.

Ramon always knew Fantasia was into new tech. She convinced him to get the new Geek Squad security system and camera set up around both grow houses. Grow house number one ran smoothly, but grow house number two had more security due to the fact she was the head of security. Fantasia was Ramon's most loyal team member.

"Well, since you have everything under control," Ramon said. "I'll go and take care of some other business."

"Yes, you know I got this over here, sweetie," Fantasia said, smiling.

Ramon headed toward the door and said, "Swing by the other house and check on everything."

"Okay, I'll stop by on my way to my mom's house."

"Thanks, Fanny?"

"It's Lori," Fantasia said, giving Ramon the finger and smiling.

Thirty minutes later, Ramon arrived at his mansion. Ten o'clock came quick and he hadn't even gotten ready for the club. He called Charles to tell him to be ready. Because tonight they were meeting up with Nisha and Vonshee.

*****

The clock had just struck ten. Nisha picked up a call that came in from Bree.

"Hello," Bree answered.

"Nisha speaking, now it's your turn," Nisha said.

"So, you're stealing phrases now?"

"No, you can keep it, Bree. What's up, beautiful?

"Are y'all almost ready? I go on stage in almost two hours."

"We're going to be there, boo. Ramon and Charles are going to meet us up there also. I invited them earlier. I'm going to make them throw money at you. You know how we do it."

"Good, they can keep J-Dub's ass busy. He acts like we're in a candy store."

Nisha laughed. "Girl, stop."

"I'm for real, Nisha. Oh shit, I have to go, my boss Henroe walking up."

Before Nisha could say anything, the phone hung up. Nisha threw her phone on her bed and turned to the mirror. She said to herself, "Well aren't you the sexiest nerd in the state of Texas. You're going to be the prettiest diva in that club tonight.

When Nisha and Vonshee arrived, they could hear the music playing loudly from the parking lot. As they approached the front door, all eyes were on them. Nisha wore a custom dress from Fendi, matching Red Bottoms with a custom red Monique Chiller purse. Vonshee wore a Calvin Klein dress, David Webb Jewelry, with blue and red Jimmy Choo heels. They both felt like superstars. After making it past the bouncer and the metal detectors, they headed to a reserved table. As they took their seats, Nisha mumbled the lyrics to 'WAP' a hit song by Cardi B. featuring Houston's own Megan Thee Stallion. The lights flashed red, blue, purple and green matching the rhythm of the beat. Moments later, Ramon and Charles walked in. Nisha noticed Ramon's clean cut features and made her way to the bar. On her way there, she noticed his Gucci shirt and matching pants. She pierced her eyes at his shoes, never seeing the brand before.

"Question," Nisha said as she and Ramon met.

"I might have an answer," Ramon replied, eyeing Nisha from head to toe.

"What kind of watch is that?" she asked, staring at the diamonds that twinkled in the light. The diamonds danced in her face.

"This is an A.P," he answered, putting the watch closer to Nisha's eyes. "Your brother sold it to me after charging me full price.

Nisha laughed. "Sounds like Cory."

"Can I buy you a drink?"

"Yes, you may," Nisha answered with a smile.

Ramon waved the bartender down and ordered his drink. The bartender turned to Nisha and asked, "And, what can I get for you, pretty lady?"

Nisha looked to the corner of her eyes. "I will have a Knock Me Out And Fuck Me. I haven't had that in a minute."

Ramon burst into a laugh. "Is that even a real drink?"

The bartender turned to Ramon with a serious look. "Coming right up."

Ramon was shocked as Nisha laughed. The drinks were made and they both made their way to VIP. Charles, Vonshee, and J-Dub were sitting and waiting for Bree's performance. The announcer announced Bree as Bree the Diva to stage. The beat to "I Need A Gansta" by Kehlani began to play through the speakers. The lights dimmed and Bree seductively walked to the stage. She twisted, turned, and rolled all over the platform. Soon, money started flying from all directions. Then she crawled on all fours and made her way to the front where her friends. were. She slowly stood up, turned around and bent over in front of Ramon. Nisha threw ones at her and Ramon followed. J-Dub cut his eyes at her, but Bree smiled and kept dancing. J-Dub smiled, then joined in. When Bree finished her set, she headed to the back while her money was swept up.

She then returned and joined her friends, sliding in next to J-Dub, eyes locked on Nisha, Bree said, "Guess what, Nisha?"

"What?"

"My boss Henroe wants to talk to you. He said it's about business. He wants you to enjoy the rest of the night first. Then, come and speak with him before we leave."

Nisha nodded with approval, putting her drink in the air.

Three hours later, the crew concluded their night of fun. Nisha left to find Henroe. She wondered what he could possibly have wanted. Then she finally located him, she introduced herself, "Ronisha, but you can just call me Nisha."

"Henry, but my people call me Henroe."

He extended his left hand. "Nice to meet you," she said, shaking his hand.

"Pleasure. So I've been informed that you have a good product."

"That could be true. Who's asking?"

Henroe laughed. "Yeah, my connection just went to the feds. So, now I'm out of a plug and now I need one. I've tested your product and it's good."

"What are you proposing?"

"I need ten pounds every two weeks. I deal with actors, athletes, ballers and people in the music business. When they come here, I try to supply them with their drug of choice. Usually weed, pills and sometimes coke."

"I can supply you with the weed. And I do have a pill connection. But I'll have to set everything up."

"That's fine with me," Henroe said. "How much are you charging?"

"Since you know Bree, I'll hook you up and charge you $2,200 a pound."

"Deal." Henroe said, extending his hand.

They exchanged numbers and arranged a meet up. As Nisha returned to her table, the club started to clear out.

"He wants to buy ten pounds every two weeks," Nisha said after returning to the table.

"Stop it." Bree said, leaving her mouth open in shock.

"You're lying," Vonshee gasped.

"I don't know, Vonshee. Nisha looks pretty truthful to me. Look at that face." Ramon said.

Everyone laughed.

"Well, I'm ready to go," Bree said.

"Yes, me too," Nisha said, yawning. "But, I'm too tipsy to drive."

"I'll be your Uber," Ramon said, shaking his keys.

Nisha gave a short stare, smiled, and agreed to the offer. "But, what about my baby?"

"I'll drive her home," Bree said. "I'll bring her to you in the morning."

"Well, let me get my bag from Quinn," Nisha said, grabbing Bree's arm.

"Who's Quinn?" Ramon laughed.

"That's what she calls her Impala," Vonshee laughed.

Nisha walked to her car with Bree, popped the trunk, and grabbed her bags that was filled with two days worth of clothes for special occasions. Ramon pulled up next to them, Nisha hopped into the car and they left. But, not before Nisha yelled out, "Later Divas!"

CHAPTER 4 – CONNECTIONS

Ramon drove though the International District of Southwest Houston. He kept his eyes on the road and came to complete stops, and was careful not to bring any attention to his vehicle. He wanted to be extra careful and he wanted to get Nisha home safe. He stopped at the light on the corner of West Airport and Fondren. He turned to Nisha, who was bobbing her head slowly to the music.

"What?" she asked, smiling and making eye contact.

"I'm waiting for you to tell me where to go from here."

"Well, Mr. Ramon, we"re going to your house. I'm spending the night with you, if that's not a problem."

The light flashed green and Ramon asked no questions as he pressed the gas pedal.

Twenty minutes later, they pulled into his garage. Nisha looked out the window and seen three other cars. a Mercedes 550, a Rolls Royce Ghost, and a GMC Denali Truck. She fell in love with the Rolls Royce.

"I didn't know you had that," Nisha said, pointing at the Ghost.

"I like to keep a simple look. Plus, I love my Challenger," Ramon said.

They went into the house through the kitchen which was attached to the garage. Ramon hung up his keys, went to the refrigerator, and poured a glass of orange juice for Nisha and himself. "Here you go," he said, pushing Nisha's drink in front of her.

"You really live here by yourself?" Nisha asked, taking a sip from her glass.

"Me and my pit-bulls."

"Yes, I met them at the grow house."

"They're good dogs,"

Nisha laughed. "Yup, and friendly."

Ramon took off his shirt. "There's a spare bathroom upstairs and down here somewhere.

"Uh, okay," Nisha said, staring at Ramon's chest.

"I'm about to go shower. Make yourself at home," Ramon said, exiting the kitchen.

Leaving Nisha by herself, she took the time to be nosey. She walked the house in curiosity. She reached a small library and opened the door. She noticed a book collection of all types of authors from James Patterson to Zane. She also found books from Robert Greene, Norie, Raquel Clarkes, Violet Blue, and even Rachael Busheel. There were even books on real-estate and how to grow your own plants. After exploring the room, a half opened safe caught her attention. She walked to it and pulled the door open. Several guns laid at the bottom, with different passports and stacks of money. Unable to control herself, Nisha opened the passport and read the name on it.

"Ramon Dumas."

She closed the safe's door and left to find a bathroom. She finally found one upstairs, and was amazed at the site. It reminded her of a MTV Crib episode. She took a bath, relaxed, got dressed, and went to find Ramon. She roamed the mansion until she found the master bedroom. Ramon was stretched out across the king size bed watching the highlights from a Houston Rockets game.

Nisha crawled into the bed with him, already knowing what she wanted. She wanted him ever since she first laid her eyes on him, she wanted all of him. She took off her shirt exposing her shape and her Savage X Fenty Lingerie by Rihanna. Ramon's eyes widened as she grabbed the remote to turn the television off. They eyed each other with an instant connection.

"Relax, I got you tonight," Nisha said, taking off his shorts and settling in between his legs with her hips in the air.

As she licked him and sucked on him, he instantly rocked up. She let her saliva drip on his manhood to lube him up. Ramon watched in amazement, then She took him deep staring in his eyes. She went up and down on him, stroking him with a hypnotizing rhythm. After showing off her skills, she pleased him until he couldn't take it any more. He ejaculated inside of her. When he exhaled and relaxed, she wiped off her lips and climbed on top of him. Sliding her panties to the side, she sat on him. Feeling every inch, she moaned. Nisha rode him until he flipped her over. Ramon was mesmerized as he penetrated her.

"Yes, Daddy," she cried out. "You feel so good."

She opened her thick legs wide. She wanted to feel all of him. Ecstasy took control as she wrapped her legs around him. Ramon stroked her slowly, then faster in missionary position as she planted her nails in his back. The sex was amazing. She felt her body enter into a different state. She knew and understood she was about to climax. Ramon was a dominant and passionate lover. He put her in multiple positions. But her favorite (like most women) was from behind. Ramon sat her up on all fours, as he pushed himself into her. He stroked, pounded, and made love to her. She moaned his name listening to her forty inch hips slap against him. He penetrated her good while pulling her hair, he smacked her buttocks.

"Oh shit, I'm about come," Ramon said.

Nisha had already reached her climax twice, she snapped back from a world of bliss and pushed him back. She positioned herself in front of him. Ramon watched in pleasure as she stroked his shaft until he came, again. Ramon's body hit the bed while Nisha collapsed next to him. He put his arms around her, panting. Nisha rubbed his chest. "Just like I thought it was going to be."

"What's that?" Ramon asked.

"Incredible," she whispered.

The next morning Nisha received a call from her sister-n-law, Karla. "Hello," Nisha answered, yawning into the phone.

"Hey Nisha," Karla said. "Sorry I missed your call."

"It's okay, I was calling to check on you and the twins."

"Oh, we're doing okay. I've just been busy moving back to Baton Rouge."

"Well, I'm glad to hear that."

"Your brother left us well off. But, I couldn't stand to be in that city knowing his killer hasn't been found. It's been hard trying to explain this to the kids."

"Trust me, I understand," Nisha said.

"I told Cory we had more than enough and he should just call it quits. But, he said he was helping so many people. He considered everybody family. So he couldn't just quit and leave everybody behind. But, you have to understand that jealousy and envy is always around you."

"Yeah, you're right about that."

"I heard about what you're doing, Nisha. I just wanted to say that I love you, please be careful, you're always welcomed into my home, the twins love you also."

Nisha let Karla vent a little bit longer. But, the comment she said about jealousy and envy kept replaying in her head.

"Well, I have to get the kids up," Karla said. "Can I call you later?"

"Yes, you can call me anytime." Nisha answered.

After the call ended, Nisha turned to Ramon, who was waking up.

"Look who decided to wake up, finally."

Ramon laughed. "Shit, I had an exciting night."

"I did too. I know it's early but I have a lot of stuff to do today. I kind of need a ride back to my apartment."

"To be honest, I have a lot of errands to run. But, you have to let me cook you breakfast first."

"Deal. You can cook while I shower," Nisha said, grabbing the sheets.

Ramon got up and headed toward the door.

"Before you go, Ramon. Can I ask you a question?"

"Sure," he said, smiling.

Knowing the answer already, she asked, "What's you last name?"

Ramon paused. "My last name is Dumas. It's French."

"Whaaat? My last name is French too."

"I think I know that, Ms. Beaudruex. Your brother was one of my best friends."

"Well, I guess yours is cute," She picked up a pillow and threw it at him.

She dropped the sheets, walked to the bathroom, and turned around to notice Ramon was watching with delight on his face. She smiled and closed the door.

Nisha was in the shower for ten minutes before her phone rang. She answered, "Hello."

"Get up, boo, " Vonshee's voice came through the speaker. "Where are you?"

"I'm still at Ramon's house."

"Well look at who was being naughty last night."

"Girl stop. And, where are you calling me from this early?"

"I just left Charles's condo," Vonshee giggled.

"And I'm the one being naughty?"

"Yup, " Vonshee said, laughing. "Have you heard from Bree? I've been calling her all morning and she hasn't answered."

"She might be on her Bonnie and Clyde shit with J-Dub."

"I thought about that, but her phone is never off."

"Her phone's off?" Nisha asked. "Well, when Ramon drops me off at home, I'll call you and you and I can swing by her crib. She still has my car."

"I forgot all about that," Vonshee said. "Call me when you make it and enjoy the rest of your morning, boo."

"Will do."

After Nisha was done upstairs, she went downstairs to the kitchen. She could smell the pancakes and bacon in the air. While Ramon had his back to her, she sat down and began to roll a blunt out of the weed bowl that was on the table.

Ramon turned around. "You are just in time. I'm almost done."

"Good, " Nisha said, licking the cigar. "Because when I'm done with this, I'm going to tear those pancakes up."

She handed the blunt to him. "Light it up."

Ramon lit it. "So, I have something to tell you."

"What's that?"

Ramon paused. "I have to catch a flight to California tomorrow."

Nisha moaned in a playful voice. "Why?"

"Family business. You know I co-own a dispensary in Cali and I have real-estate out there. I'll be back in a week."

Nisha gave him puppy dog eyes. "So, I have to wait to get some more D?"

Ramon laughed. "I'll make it up to you, I promise."

"You better, because it was too good."

"I will," Ramon said, putting, her food in front of her. "Now eat."

Nisha looked up at him, grabbed her fork, and said, "Yes, Daddy."

An hour later, Nisha was back at her apartment when She received a text from Bree.

"Where are you? I'm about to bring you your car," Nisha read out loud.

Nisha called her after seeing the text.

"Bree speaking, now it's your turn."

"Where have you been?" Nisha asked with a slight attitude.

"Sleep, that's what people usually do after they've had a long, night at a strip club."

"You made us worry. Plus, your phone was off."

"It died and I was tired. I forgot to plug it in last night."

"Oh, okay."

"Where are you? So I can bring you your car."

"I'm at home," Nisha answered.

"I'll be there in ten minutes."

"Cool," Nisha said, lookin, at her phone. "I have a customer calling, Vonshee is on her way also. Are you Bonnie and Clyding today or are you riding with us?"

"I can ride. Jay said he had something to do today."

"Cool, we're going to the Academy Store today."

"Why?" Bree asked.

"Because, I want to buy a gun."

"Are you serious?"

"I'm dead serious and my customer just hung up. He'll call back."

"Well, looks like we're all about to get one. I want one too and I know Vonshee is going to want one."

"We have to have protection. Call me when you're pulling up."

When Nisha hung up, she sat back on her sofa, relaxed, and thought about Ramon. He made her feel special. She likes everything about him so she made the decision, from now on she would be his Ride or Die Bitch.

CHAPTER 5 – THE SCENE

The lyrics from Rocko Main1's song "Don't Make A Scene" blasted through the speakers of Nisha's Alpine system. She always compared him to modern day Tupac. It had been days since she heard from Ramon. But she was always doing business transactions, so her mind was always occupied. Plus, today she was meeting Henroe the club's manager. They were meeting at a discreet location. Bree tagged along and Charles followed behind in another car. After arriving, Nisha pulled into the parking lot. Henroe stood outside a car with another man.

"Who was he?' Nisha thought to herself.

"Hello, Nisha," Henroe began. "This is my business partner, Briscoe."

"Oh, nice to meet you, Briscoe," she said, offering her hand.

She turned to Henroe. "You have my money?"

Henroe smiled. "You have my product?"

Nisha waved to Bree. Bree slowly walked up carrying two duffle bags and dropped them at Henroe's Smoke Grey Jondans. She opened them, showing five pounds in each bag. Henroe asked Briscoe to grab the suitcase.

Briscoe returned and opened the suitcase, which revealed $20,000 staring at Nisha. Nisha eyed rolls of money assuming it was due to the fact that he worked at a gentlemen's club.

"It's all there, and if it's not, you know where to find me," Henroe said.

Nisha grabbed the suitcase. "It was nice doing business with you. I hope we can do more in the future."

Henroe smiled. "Likewise."

Nisha shook Henroe's hand, turned away, and walked to her car with Bree.

After they were in the vehicle, Bree asked, "What do you think about that?"

"Smooth, " Nisha replied, grinning.

"It was like a movie scene."

Both women Laughed as Nisha pulled away, feeling special, like a true dope girl. She popped in "The Port of Miami" an album by self-proclaimed drug dealer turned rapper, Rick Ross.

Nisha dropped off Bree and headed to Vonshee at the smoke shop. When she arrived, Vonshee stood outside, smoking and leaning against a wall. Nisha walked over and yelled, "Yo, Smokey. You smoking my shit?"

Vonshee burst into a laugh and said, "Rule number five. Never get high on your own supply."

They giggled and walked inside. Nisha followed Vonshee to the back of the smoke shop. Vonshee had asked a coworker to cover for her.

"What brings you here to see me?" Vonshee asked.

"Girl stop. " Nisha grinned.

"Vonshee ginned, as she was reaching, into her purse. She pulled out a roll of cash. She then unwrapped a thick rubber band and unfolded a bundle of money. "You must've came for this?"

Nisha laughed. "Actually, I didn't. But, since you're bringing money up."

"You can count it but, I counted it multiple times and it's all there. I charged $15 a gram."

"You gram for gram your whole pound?"

"Yup, " Vonshee said. "Wasn't that the plan?"

"I mean, I guess."

"Matter of fact, just take my cut and reinvest it," Vonshee said, handing Nisha another roll of money.

"Are you serious?"

"Yeah, we're trying to be like Trump's hair piece rich."

Nisha smirked. "Well, I need to go re-up anyway. Ramon told Charles to tell me to go pick up from the second grow house."

"Cool, I have to get back to work. I'll swing by your spot later, if it's cool with you."

"That's fine with me," Nisha said, putting the money in her purse. Nisha left the smoke shop, jumped on Highway 59, and headed toward the second grow house. When she arrived, she grabbed her purse and walked to the door.

The door opened. "Diva," Charles jokingly said, putting his hands in the air.

"This is where you came after we left Henroe?" Nisha asked.

"Yup, Ramon said to get your re-up here. So, I had to come here, duh. Fantasia already had everything ready."

"Who's Fantasia?"

"Damn, you never met, Lori?" Charles asked. "That's crazy but, she's our tech, and a badass hacker."

"Really?"

"She could get through anything. Ramon's friendly nerd. I'll introduce y'all and she'll do the rest," Charles laughed.

Nisha smiled.

Charles called Fantasia to meet Nisha.

"Hello," Fantasia said, waving and walking in the room. "I heard that too, Charles."

"Hello, I'm Nisha," Nisha said, extending her hand.

"I'm Lori, but everyone calls me Fantasia. I'm pretty sure you know why."

Nisha tilted her head. "Is it because you look like her."

"Yes, and I get that a lot, but I don't mind. Ramon gave me the nickname. And, it just kind of stuck."

"Really? How long have you known Ramon?"

"Almost ten years."

"Well, it's nice to finally meet you. As you know, I'm here to re-up."

"Yup, follow me," Fantasia said.

Nisha handed Charles her re-up money as they all walked into the packing room. "Question, Charles?" she asked.

"Ask," he responded, putting a stack of money in the money counter.

"I've re-upped twice already. Can my crew and I get a larger front?"

Charles squinted at Nisha. "If you believe your crew can handle it, we can double up, I suppose."

"Well, here's some extra funds," Nisha said, handing him more money.

Nisha and Charles packed the vacuum sealed packages into two duffle bags. They headed toward the front door, when Fantasia stopped them.

"I'll walk her," Fantasia said, grabbing a bag from Charles. "I'm headed to my mom's house."

After reaching Nisha's car, Nisha asked, "So, you're the operation's tech?"

"Yeah, something like head of security," Fantasia responded. "Nothing gets a hundred yards to the front door without me knowing. I used to work for Geek Squad. My ex-boyfriend there showed me how to hack. I guess you can say something good came out of the relationship."

"For real?" Nisha asked.

While Fantasia gave a little more detail about herself. Nisha had been hit with an idea to ask Fantasia to be a part of her crew, the Pretty Divas.

"What are you doing later tonight?" Nisha asked.

"Nothing, why?"

"Would you mind joining me and my girls to an all girls night out?"

Fantasia paused. "I'd love to."

"Good, I'll text you," Nisha said, handing her phone to Fantasia.

Fantasia programmed her number and handed the phone back. "Text me."

"I will."

Before Nisha drove off, Fantasia stuck her hand through the window. "It was really nice to meet you, Nisha."

Nisha shook her hand, smiled and said, "It was my pleasure."

Hours later, Nisha's phone rang. It was Vonshee. "Hey, sexy," Vonshee answered.

"Hey, I had a revelation." Nisha began, "Pretty Divas has only three members. I want to grow and make us bigger. We moved twenty pounds this week. Imagine what we could do if we had a crew as big as Ramon's."

"Okay, slow down Ms. Scarface," Vonshee joked.

"I'm for real. We could be big. An all girls crew that moves major weed."

"Look, whatever you are with, I'm with," Vonshee said.

"I'm for real. And I'm glad to hear that, boo. Oh shit, Ramon's calling me. Let me call you back later."

Nisha clicked over, "Hey, Daddy!"

"Hey, what have you been up to, pretty lady?" Ramon asked.

"Making money."

"I've been hearing," Ramon laughed.

"You have?"

"Yup, but I also have some bad news."

"Awww," she mumbled. "What is it?"

"I have to stay out here for another week."

"Are you serious?" Nisha asked, stopping at a red light.

"Yeah, I promise I'll make it up to you."

"You better," Nisha laughed. "Making me go without your sex. Are you crazy?"

"A little bit," Ramon answered.

"Well, we're going out tonight. All the girls, including Fantasia. You don't mind me inviting your tech girl?"

"That's cool with me,"

Ramon said. "I'll call you later when I make it back to my sister's house."

"Okay," Nisha said, pulling away from the light and hanging up. Nisha called Bree and told her that she had a surprise after she performed tonight. She also told her to come by before she left for work, so she could give her another pound to sell. At eleven sharp, Nisha and Vonshee walked through D-Live. Nisha could tell from the moment she walked in, the club had a different vibe. This night was different from last. She even thought she saw James Harden. Vonshee made her way to the bar to order drinks and a stack of 1,000 ones. When she made her way back to Nisha, Nisha was texting.

"Who are you texting?" Bree asked.

"Oh, nobody, just a friend," Nisha answered.

"Yeah, a friend, okay, Nisha."

Minutes later, Bree the Diva was announced to the stage. The lights dimmed and flashed. The beat to "Sex With Me," a song by Rihanna, blast through the speakers. Bree slowly walked to the stage. She usually did one slow sexy song and two or three twerk songs. The regulars loved it. Nisha knew her friend loved to dance, especially in front of a crowd. So, it came to no surprise when she found out Bree was dancing at a strip club. And, Bree always went crazy when she knew her crew was there. Nisha and Vonshee would throw 1,000 ones to cause a ripple effect, forcing all the ballers to throw their money. And, it worked all the time.

After Bree's show, she would exit the stage, get dressed and head over to her friends at their reserved table for the rest of the night.

Nisha took a sip from her drink as Bree sat next to her.

"That was the bomb," Vonshee said.

"Thanks, that was for you two," Bree laughed, pointing at both ladies.

Fantasia caught Nisha's eyes when she walked through the club.

Nisha excused herself and left to go get her. When she returned she said, "Okay Divas, this is my surprise I promised you both. This is Ramon's tech, Fantasia."

"Damn."

"Bree said." Has anyone ever told you that you look like-"

"Yes," Fantasia said. "My real name is Lori, but people call me that because I look like her."

"Like a short version," Vonshee said. "But, you could be her sister."

Bree laughed. "You could really confuse people."

"Only in pictures, she's way much taller," Nisha said. "Have a seat."

Nisha noticed Bree's attention shifted, but she kept talking. "So, I want my Pretty Diva Crew to expand. And, I want my first recruit to be Fantasia. Only if she accepts."

Vonshee spit out her drink as she took a sip. "Are you drunk, Nisha?"

"Nope, I know this is Ramon's tech. I'll handle him and I'm sure that everything will be okay."

Bree turned her head back to the table.

"If you say so."

"So, do you want to be down, Fantasia? Nisha asked. "We need you to be apart of this all female empire."

Shocked for a moment. "How could I deny an offer like that? I can handle both jobs. Ramon won't even notice I'm gone," Fantasia said with a smile.

"Well, it's an honor to have you." Nisha said.

All the girls nodded in approval.

Seconds later, Nisha noticed Bree looking at J-Dub getting flirty with a dancer. Bree excused herself.

"Oh no you don't, Bree. I'm going with you. Excuse us." Nisha said.

Nisha followed Bree, hoping to calm her down before she made a scene.

"So, you're just going to be disrespectful in front of me? And, what are you even doing here tonight, Jay?" Bree asked, after they reached J-Dub.

"I ain't doing shit," J-Dub responded. "I was just having a conversation."

"It looks like you're flirting with this hoe, Diamond."

Diamond walked away to avoid trouble.

"Bree, you're making a scene." J-Dub laughed.

Nisha could sense Bree's anger, so she grabbed her. By then, Henroe also walked up after he noticed the tension and awkwardness. He put his arm around Bree. "You're too pretty to be getting mad like this. Talk with me. I have some business to discuss with you."

"Yeah, do what your boss says." J-Dub laughed.

Nisha couldn't control herself as she slapped J-Dub across the face. "Oh my God, you're such an ass."

J-Dub grabbed his face and laughed. "You got that one, Nisha."

"Are you fucking threatening me?" Nisha asked with an attitude.

"Naw, I'd never do that."

"You're such an ass. I don't even know how my brother dealt with you." Nisha stared at him before she turned around and walked away.

"What was that?" Vonshee asked as Nisha took her seat.

"I couldn't help myself. He was being an ass to Bree."

The girls tried to enjoy the rest of their night but Nisha was so angry, she decided to call it an early night. The parking lot was filled with activity.

Bree approached Nisha as she was getting into her Impala. "J-Dub was my ride. I didn't drive my car, so can I go home with you tonight?"

"Sure, you're always welcomed. I thought you were gonna go ballistic earlier."

Bree smiled. "Pretty Divas don't get mad and cause a scene. We just get even."

Nisha laughed. "Okay, well, get in so we can get the hell out of here."

CHAPTER 6 – GETTING EVEN

A week had gone by before Nisha headed back to her daily routine supplying quarters, a half, and a whole pound of weed became her new favorite thing to do. Her best customer, Henroe the club manager, requested ten pounds every two weeks.

Nisha parked in a Wal-Mart parking lot, thinking, calculating in her head, if she kept at her current pace, she could make $375,000 at a minimum. Plus, whatever her crew brought in. That would easily bring them to half a million in their first year of dealing. "Not bad for a new dope girl," she said to herself.

Her plan was to sell until she reached a target amount. Then she would quit. She understood that most drug dealers got caught and headed to the feds because of greed. Plus, they never developed an exit plan.

Nisha's thoughts were interrupted by call from Ramon.

"Hey, you," Nisha answered.

"What are you doing?" Ramon asked.

"My rounds," Nisha said. "What about you, boo?"

"You've been calling me boo and babe lately. Are we a couple?"

Nisha laughed. "I thought you knew this?"

"When did this happen?"

"When you got you some," Nisha laughed.

"That's what I'm talking about. A woman who knows what she wants."

"Yup," Nisha laughed. "And, I'm building a bigger and better crew. I even asked Fantasia to join the Pretty Divas."

"And, how's that's working out?" Ramon asked.

"You know she's over my security and she's my tech?"

"She's a big girl, Fantasia can handle it. We're all in this together, right? We all should be good."

"Yes, we are. I'll be back tomorrow. Pick me up from the airport at one. We can talk about this after I'm home."

"Great, I can't wait."

Moments later, Nisha called Vonshee. Nisha knew it was Vonshee's day off. So, she decided to visit her.

Vonshee was sitting in her front yard when Nisha pulled up. Vonshee waved as she hopped out of her Impala. After greeting each other, they went inside.

"What brings you to these parts?" Vonshee asked.

"Bored. Plus I have no man to go home to."

"That won't be long," Vonshee joked.

Nisha smirked. "Yeah, he said he'll be here tomorrow."

"Honestly, it sounds like you're falling for him."

"He is different," Nisha said. "Remember that bullshit dude, Q?"

"How could I not? He was so lame," Vonshee laughed. "I never liked his ass."

They both laughed as Nisha reached into her purse, pulling out $5,000.

"Here, this is for you."

"For what?" Vonshee asked, eyeing the money.

"Your cut and a little extra for being such a good friend," Nisha said.

"I have been a ride or die chick since high school, haven't I?"

Nisha and Vonshee became best friends in high school. One morning, Nisha turned a corner going to class. Nisha witnessed Vonshee and Carlos, a guy from the Pines of Westbury, getting into a heated argument. Carlos roughed her up because Vonshee was seen talking to a guy he didn't like. Nisha ran over and pushed Carlos and yelled, "Don't fucking put your hands on her." Carlos stumbled to the ground, got up angry, and walked off, probably knowing he couldn't put his hands on Cory's nerdy little sister. Students saw what had happened and word spread like wildfires. Nisha instantly became popular. The whole student body wanted to be the curvy nerd's friend. But it was Vonshee and Bree who became the closest.

Nisha waved her hands in front of Vonshee's face. "You okay?" Nisha asked. "You left me for a minute there."

Vonshee laughed. "My bad, I went back to high school at Westbury."

"Oh, well, I said, do you think we're going to make it far?"

"Hell yeah! Especially with your smart ass leading us and Ramon backing us up."

"Karla told me to be careful because envy and jealousy is always around. That shit stuck with me."

Vonshee pulled her phone out. "Well, I got your back. If any envious bitches come at us, they're going down. Just be sure you have the money to bail me out. I ain't trying to be sleeping with no rats."

Nisha laughed. "You worried about a four legged rat? We need to be worried about these rats walking around here on two feet."

Vonshee burst into a laughter. "Girl stop."

"I'm for real!"

"We sell weed," Vonshee said. "What's the worst that could happen? All I know this, we're making a lot of money. So, let's just enjoy it. Anything goes sideways, we leave. Me, you and Bree." Vonshee said, pointing at Nisha's phone as it rang.

"It does feel good making this kind of money," Nisha said, picking up her phone and swiping the call button.

"Hello. Yeah, I have some," Nisha said. "I can be there in fifteen."

Nisha hung up and turned to her friend. "I have to go."

"It's cool," Vonshee said, making puppy dog eyes.

"Chacho's tonight. Call Bree and tell her," Nisha said, walking out the front door.

*****

Bree was on all fours at Henroe's condo. He pounded her from behind, gripping her hips and plowing her intensely. They were dripping wet like it was a hundred degrees outside. Bree was feeling so good that her moans couldn't even leave her mouth. She knew Henroe had always wanted to have sex with her. She stood five foot four with an amazing body. She knew he was trying to make a good first impression also. He brought her to new heights. His strokes were unmatched to anyone she had ever slept with, including J-Dub. Bree came repeatedly. He was penetrating her like he had something to prove. Feeling him about to burst, she started rocking harder to match his thrust. Henroe backed out of her and unloaded.

"That's how you get even," Bree whispered.

"What?" Henroe said, breathing hard.

"Nothing," she smiled.

"Yeah, whatever," Henroe said. "I got to go to the bathroom."

Resting on Henroe's bed. Bree thought about the time she went through J-Dub's phone. She had seen his sexual encounter with her co-worker, Diamond. She'd never said anything about it, because she loved him and their Bonnie and Clyde act. But after seeing him and her flirt with each other, she had reached her limit and knew exactly how she was going to get back at him.

Sleeping with her boss had always crossed her mind.

Bree's phone rang, snapping her out of her thoughts.

Bree speaking, now it's your turn," she said.

Nisha laughed. "Girl's Night. Meet us at Chacho's at eight."

"Okay, I'll be there."

"Whoa, why do you sound like you're out of breath? You know what, never mind. Ramon is coming back tomorrow so I get it." Nisha laughed and hung up.

CHAPTER 7 - WHERE IS SHE?

The plane hadn't fully arrived at the gate before Ramon dashed down the aisle. While waiting for his checked bags, he phoned Charles.

"What's good, Maine?" Charles answered.

"Is everything running smoothly? Tell me what I missed."

"Well, a couple of people have been short and it's been hard to get in touch with some folks, fights here and there, that's about it."

"Call everybody and tell them to be at the second grow house at six tonight."

"I got you. You need me to pick you up?"

"Naw, I'm good. Nisha's pulling up right now. I will call you in few."

Ramon loaded his things in the car as Nisha jumped out and ran to him. She gave him a welcoming kiss. Ramon gripped her from behind.

"I missed you, " Nisha said.

"I missed your Beyoncé looking ass too."

Nisha Laughed, hitting his chest. "I don't look like her."

An hour later, Nisha and Ramon were at his mansion in Sugarland, Texas.

Ramon sat on his sofa and closed his eyes. Nisha joined him as they drifted off holding each other. Nisha was happy to be in her man's arms again.

At six, Ramon's meeting was in process. He stood up at the head of the table. "I've called this meeting today to discuss some things. From what I've been hearing, we have been short on money and been out of contact. We have a lot of shitty issues going on that's fucking with this operation. I have a problem with that and when shit like that fucks with my money, then I got a big fucking issue with that. When people can't be reached or they're coming up short on their cash. Then I'm short. And, that shit ain't good for business, my business. So now we have to switch up some shit. From now on, if you need to re-up, it will be done through Charles. If you short, don't even come around. If your relationship is having issues, keep it away from my place of business. And, if you have a problem with that, then get the fuck out of my operation."

Ramon finished and stormed out, leaving stunned crew members staring at one another.

Ramon entered into his Hellcat, closing the door, he seen Nisha and Fantasia in his window.

"So, you call yourself being mean," Nisha said.

Ramon laughed after trying to look serious. "So, I heard you're a Pretty Diva now?'" he said to Fantasia.

"Yes," Fantasia replied, smiling and giving Nisha an elbow bump.

He grinned. "Well, just look after one another."

"We will." Nisha said.

"Good," he said as he glanced at J-Dub's Challenger, shaking his head. He put his car into drive but, not before Nisha kissed him goodbye.

"I'll ride with Bree and Jay. They're going my way." Nisha said before leaving.

*****

The next morning, Nisha woke up well rested. Not remembering what time she fell asleep, she missed calls from Ramon, Vonshee, Bree, and Henroe. "I'll call everyone after I get ready," she said to herself, yawning.

Before she put a foot in the shower, her phone went off. Glancing at it, she realized it was a text. It was from a number she didn't recognize.

The text read: So, you think you're hot shit. You think just because you came up in a short time that you're better than us. Well, remember what goes up must come down. And, every empire comes to a tragic end.

Nisha re-read the text to make sure she was reading it correctly. She decided to forward it to Fantasia.

Minutes later, Fantasia called. "Was that a real text?"

"Yes. Do you think you can trace it?"

"When did you get it?" Fantasia asked.

"Minutes ago."

"I can try. But, these days there's all kinds of apps and stuff out here. That could've come from anywhere. Bring me your phone so I can run some of my reverse software on it."

"Text me your address and I'll be on my way."

Later Nisha's eyes were on Fantasia working her magic. Fantasia typed away at her laptop, then leaned back into her chair. "Yup, just as I suspected. It's from a Text Me app."

Nisha knew the answer but she asked anyway, "What's a Text Me app?"

"It's a downloadable app that allows you to hide your number, send texts, and call as a different number. But it's limited."

"Can you find out what number it's linked to?" Nisha asked.

Fantasia cracked her knuckles. "Yes, but it'll take some time. I should be able to find an IP address."

"Well, take your time. But, I want to know whose number that is."

"I'll work my jelly," Fantasia said.

"I have to go take care of some business. Please keep me updated."

Walking out the door, Nisha called Henroe to schedule their weekly meeting. She told him to meet her at Lotus, a Louisiana cajun style restaurant that achieved fame after rappers started mentioning them in their songs.

Pulling into the parking lot, she parked next to Henroe's Audi A8. After greeting each other, Henroe said, "Your weed is a hit. Everyone wants it."

Nisha laughed. "Tell me something I don't know."

The transaction was quick, they ordered to-go meals, then left. Nisha arrived at the light on Bellfort and Fondren. She called Karla and agreed to visit her this Friday. After her call with Karla, she called Ramon.

"What's up, sexy," he answered.

"Sorry I missed your call last night. I was tired."

"It's okay, I called it an early night also."

They talked a little bit longer then hung up, but not before planning a dinner together. She stopped at the next light and thought about Cory, staring at her Glock 17 she bought from Academy. 'I promise I'll kill whoever murdered you, I will avenge you big brother.' Her thinking of revenge came to an end when the car behind honked. The light was green so she sped off down West Bellfort.

Hours passed and Nisha and Ramon were at a restaurant she never even heard of before. She told him everything that happened that morning. Ramon blew it off and said don't worry about it.

"Oh, I almost forgot. I'm leaving to go see the twins and Karla. Do you want to come?" Nisha asked.

Ramon looked up from his steak. "You know I have to stay here, Nisha. Maybe next time."

"Okay," Nisha said with a disappointing face.

"It's kind of messed up that I just got back and you want to leave."

"I'm sorry, babe. But, you know I haven't seen them in a long time."

"Naw, it's okay. Tell Karla if she needs anything to hit me up."

Nisha smiled. "Yes, Daddy."

Ramon thought about Nisha many times after she left. But tonight, he was ready to have some fun. He invited all of his workers to D-Live. At eleven, he met Charles and J-Dub at the night club. By midnight they were slamming shots. They headed to VIP and met Vonshee and Fantasia.

"Has anyone heard from Bree?" Vonshee asked, staring at J-Dub.

J-Dub grinned. "Haven't heard from her since Monday."

"This is her night to dance, so we might see her," Ramon said.

Fantasia tapped Ramon's shoulder. "Can I speak with you alone?"

They strolled over to the bar. Fantasia had concern on her face. "Nisha and Vonshee received some weird texts this week. Vonshee told me she got hers two days ago. At first I thought nothing of it. I told Nisha I would look into it and I did but what found was crazy. I tracked that Text App and the IP address back to-"

"Back to where?"' Ramon asked.

"Back to Bree's phone."

"What?" he laughed.

"That can't be right."

"Trust me, Ramon. It's right.

Ramon put his hand on his chin. "Whatever you do, don't tell, Nisha."

"What?"

"You heard me, Fanny," he responded with an attitude.

"Okay, okay," Fantasia said, putting her hands up.

On their way back to VIP, Ramon asked, "Can you find a good location to put a hair salon at?"

"Yeah, but why?"

"Nisha's birthday is in a couple of weeks, I'm thinking of investing in a hair salon for her to wash her money through."

When they returned, Ramon noticed J-Dub was missing. "Where's J-Dub?"

"I think he went looking for Bree," Charles said, bobbing his head to the music.

Hours passed and there was no sign of Bree. Ramon stumbled through the half empty club on his way to the men's room.

"Fuck," he said as his phone vibrated.

"Hello," he answered, unzipping his pants to urinate.

"So, you're ignoring my calls now?" Nisha's voice pierced his ears loudly and cold.

"Naw, I just didn't hear it or feel it ringing. You know it's loud here."

"Yeah, whatever," she said. "I heard you was at the bar with Fantasia for a little longer than needed."

"Who told you that?" Ramon asked, zipping up his fly.

"Who else, nigga."

"Why are you tripping?" Ramon said. "It was strictly business."

"Well, I'm out here until Monday. Try not to get into no bullshit while I'm gone."

"Let's get something straight, Nisha. I wear the pants in this relationship," he said. "And, have you seen Bree?"

"What the hell?" Nisha shouted.

"Why are you asking me about another bitch?"

Controlling his attitude, he answered, "Because no one has heard from her or seen her. I'm asking you because she's one of your best friends."

"Well, I haven't spoken to her, nor even seen her."

"How well do you know her?"

"What the fuck?" Nisha huffed."

"Are you kidding me?"

"I'm just asking," Ramon said.

"You know what, Ramon? I'm about to hang up before I curse you out. You have to be drunk right now."

Unfazed by the conversation, Ramon drove home safely and passed out in his king size bed.

*****

Monday crept up fast. Nisha called Vonshee to ask if she seen Bree.

"I haven't heard from her," Vonshee answered.

"This isn't like her. I've been calling and only her voicemail answers. Then Ramon asking all these questions about her."

While Vonshee talked, Nisha was hit with an idea, one that would get some answers quick. "Let me call you back, Vonshee," she said as she hung up.

Nisha phoned Ramon twice before he answered.

"Where are you? I'm home and I want to see you," she said in a sexy tone.

"I'm on the west. I can be there in fifteen minutes," Ramon said.

"You know I've been waiting on your sexy ass."

"Well, hurry up because I'm horny."

Ramon made it there in ten minutes. He parked his Hellcat and knocked on Nisha's door. She answered, just wearing a bra and panties. They kissed long and passionately like two lovers who haven't. seen each other in years. Ramon grabbed her thick flesh and picked her up, carried her into the room, and the sudden comfort of the bed put them away. Ramon removed her panties and held both her legs up to her shoulders. His tongue touched her swollen clit.

While he licked and pulled. Nisha felt ecstasy. "Yes, Daddy! It feels so damn good," she moaned. Ramon noticed her eyes rolling to the back of her head, he stood and stripped off all of his clothes. He turned Nisha over and licked her slowly from behind, until he reached her lower back. "Yes Ramon, I like it," she told him, sitting up on all fours. She rocked back and forward off his tongue until she came. Her body hit the mattress. Flipping over, she spread her legs open and told him to make love to her. Ramon slid in and began to pump slowly. Feeling Nisha squeeze her thick thighs around him only encouraged him to pump harder. She was enormously wet from back to back orgasms. She accommodated his girth as she kissed him, moaned, and grind her hips. Placing her D-cup breast in his mouth, he bit her nipple.

Nisha gasped, "Yes, Daddy." Wanting to ride his shaft, she got on top grabbing all eight inches of his manhood. She slid down on it slowly and wiggled her hips. She moaned in pleasure as she bounced up and down. She took the pain with a bliss. Ramon grabbed her hips trying to thrust harder. And, right before he was about to bust, Nisha reached under her pillow, grabbed her Glock, and stuffed it in Ramon's face.

"What the fuck?" he yelled, putting his hands up.

Tears came down Nisha's face. "Ramon, are you fucking around on me?"

"Are you fucking serious?"

"Are you fucking with Fantasia or Bree?"

Trying to dodge the barrel of her pistol, he asked. "What are you talking about, babe? I would never do that."

"Don't fucking babe me. Just answer the question," she cried. "You stopped answering your phone and you started acting all weird and shit. You must think I'm stupid."

Ramon wide eyed the Glock. "First off, I'm not cheating on you. Bree is missing, nobody has seen or heard from her. Fantasia said you and Vonshee was getting weird texts. She pulled me to the side to tell me that she tracked the texts back to…"

Nisha waved the gun in his face. "Back to where?"

Ramon paused. "Back to Bree's phone."

Nisha was stunned and Ramon took the split second to snatch the gun away from her. He dropped the clip and smiled, seeing that there were no bullets in it.

Nisha grabbed the sheets and rolled off of him. "I'm sorry, Ramon. If you want to leave and never talk to me again, I'll understand."

Ramon stared at her, then put his arms around her. He told her he could understand everything she's been going through lately. But, pulling a gun on him was uncalled for.

Moments later, Ramon's phone rang. He glanced at it and saw it was Fantasia.

Nisha gave a look to assure him it was okay to answer.

"Hello," he said, putting his phone on speaker.

"Where are you, Ramon?" Fantasia asked.

"At Nisha's. Why?"

"You need to get to the first weed house, fast."

"Why?" Ramon answered.

Fantasia took a deep breath. "Because growth house number one is currently on fire."

Ramon stood up. "What? Where is everybody?"

"That's a good question. I went by to check the security system, I smelled burning marijuana from a block away, I turned down Silo Street and saw flames in the air."

"Where are you?" Nisha asked Fantasia.

"I'm down the street, watching. The fire department just pulled up. I was gonna go and get a closer look, but..."

"But, what?" Ramon asked.

Fantasia paused. "There's cops. A lot of them."

"Ok, stay there," Ramon said. "We're on our way."

CHAPTER 8 - WILDFIRES

Nisha and Ramon entered the neighborhood, staring at the grow house, as it burnt to the ground. Ramon drove his Denali Truck past the scene. Knowing people would recognize his Challenger, he chose to switch vehicles. Firefighters and police officers were everywhere. And what made things worse, the Channel 2 News pulled up. You could definitely smell weed blocks away.

"I know everybody out here is high," Nisha said with a smirk.

Ramon laughed, even though the matter was serious.

"Who is that?" Nisha asked, pointing at a middle age woman stepping out of an unmarked crown vic.

The woman was Detective Lopez, a five foot seven hard-nose by the book detective, who was determined to excel in her career. Nisha also noticed a younger caramel skin woman exiting the car. She could only assume the younger female was her rookie partner, but the woman seemed so familiar.

Ramon also noticed. "Damn," he said. "Fucking Detectives."

While the flames were being put out, Ramon phoned Fantasia, who was parked down the street. "Tell everyone to meet me at the second grow house tomorrow at ten a.m. sharp," he said, driving off.

The next morning, Nisha and Ramon were sitting in the living room of the grow house. Ramon waited for every member of his crew to show up before he began. J-Dub and others were fifteen minutes late.

"Sorry we're late." J-Dub said. "I had to pick Rasheem up on the way here."

"Where's Bree?" Vonshee asked J-Dub.

Shrugging his shoulders. "I have not seen her honestly,"

Clearing his throat, Ramon cut in. "Look, everyone should know by now that house number one has been burnt down. And, if I find that anybody from this crew had anything to do with it, they'll be dealt with. But, right now, I can't assume anything. Half of our product has just been destroyed. Which means, half of our profits are gone. Luckily the house was in Cory's name."

"Who's name is this house in?" Nisha asked.

"Cory's," Ramon said. "Which means we need to find a new location, fast."

"We need to make coke our number one product. We can double up faster," J-Dub said.

Charles responded. "I'll have to agree with Jay."

"What's up with you guys and this coke shit," Nisha said. "Look, we just lost a house. So, now we need an one stop shop for everything, like a nice size warehouse or something."

Everyone stared at Nisha like the genius she was.

"That's a great idea." Ramon smiled.

"I can link you up with my homegirl, Delilah, she's into commercial real-estate." Fantasia said.

Ramon nodded. "Cool, make it happen."

Yes, sir," Fantasia said, giving him the thumbs up.

"Look, even though we only move weed and pills. We have to remember we move a very large amount. Cops and detectives will be on to us now. So, I want everyone to fly low for right now. That includes you and your crew, Nisha."

Nisha nodded in agreement.

Before Ramon closed his meeting, he turned to Fantasia. "Do me two favors. First, find out what happened to our grow house. And, number two, locate Bree, asap."

*****

A week had gone by and no one heard from Bree nor any info on the grow house. Feeling like Sherlock, Fantasia woke up and called Nisha. "You want to ride with me? I'm going to the grow house scene."

"Sure," Nisha answered.

"Okay, I'll pick you up in a hour," Fantasia said. "Send me your address and I'll be on my way."

They pulled up to the neighborhood of South Meadow. They both jumped out in professional attires and clipboards to look like estimators from an insurance company. They walked around in what was left of the house. The smell of marijuana still lingered. Fantasia noticed tables made of heavy metal missing and camera equipment were burned up everywhere.

"Someone wants us to suffer," Nisha said.

"I agree," Fantasia said with a frown, picking up a glass bottle with her pen.

"I think we should leave. This doesn't feel right."

"Yeah, let's go," Fantasia agreed.

On the way out, Nisha noticed a silver box peeking from under debris.

"What is this?" Nisha asked, grabbing the box. Fantasia strolled over.

"That's a titanium hard drive I hooked the computer to. The ports are burned out, but the memory chip is good. I can send it to my Geek Squad buddy and have him refurbish it. Then I'll be able to see what's on it."

"It still looks like it's in good condition," Nisha said, turning it around and flipping it upside down.

"Guess it was lucky."

Both women got into the car, Fantasia pulled off and seconds later a car followed. Fantasia made several stops before she noticed the same vehicle in her rearview mirror. She adjusted her mirror for a better view, then pressed the gas pedal harder, to ease away. Soon the car made a quick right down another street.

"It seemed like someone was following us," Fantasia said to Nisha.

Turning around in the front seat. "Are you serious?" Nisha asked.

"Maybe or maybe I'm being paranoid."

"Or maybe not," Nisha said, fixing her side mirror.

*****

Ramon stood in a Wal-Mart parking lot admiring his GMC Denali Truck, the 26 inches Lorenzos looked great, the black custom paint with silver specs made the truck twinkle in the light. Large fog lights were mounted along the top of the roof that could light up a large ranch. He also had a custom Dewalt toolbox installed with a hidden compartment where he kept his AK-47 for emergencies. Artillery was a must in Houston.

Ramon's phone rang while he drove from the parking lot. "Hello."

"Hmm, Yes. Is this Mr. Dumas?" the caller asked.

"Yes, it is. Who is this?"

"My name is Delilah Shea. I was given your number by Lori Johnson."

"Yeah, I know her," he said, referring to Fantasia's real name.

"Good," Delilah said. "I was informed you were trying to buy a warehouse as soon as possible. Is that correct?"

"Yes, it is ma'am."

Delilah laughed. "Please, call me, Delilah."

"Okay." Ramon replied

"Well, I found a warehouse close to the Port of Houston. It's 15,000 square feet. I can meet you there so you can view it, if it's possible."

"No, that won't be necessary. I need that building like, Yesterday."

"Okay, so what do you need from me?"

"I need for you to start all the paperwork work and provide me with keys to the building. I can wire the money to whoever right now."

"I can do that for you," Delilah began, "I'll text you all the information you need. When everything goes through, I'll bring you the keys."

"Sounds good to me," Ramon replied.

"I'm sending all the information to you right now."

"Great, and before you go, if it's possible can you find me a location for a hair salon?"

"Yes, I actually have one on the market right now."

"Good, I want it also," Ramon said, zooming through a yellow light.

CHAPTER 9 – PRETTY DIVAS

July came fast and Ramon was a very busy man. He had just lost one of his grow houses, bought a warehouse, relocated everything, reconstructed his businesses, and even put together a salon for Nisha. The salon had it all from new appliances, new chairs, mirrors, flatscreens and marble installed sinks for shampooing. Fantasia even hooked up the latest Geek Squad Business Security System.

Today was a special day. His girlfriend's 28th birthday and his plan was to surprise her with her own beauty salon.

Ramon called Nisha and asked her to be ready at six so they could make the reservation at Grand Lucks. After hanging up, Ramon's sister called.

"Hello," he answered, making a right down West Airport.

"Ramon, you need to get back to California quick," his sister said.

"Why? What happened?"

"Mama, she's sick. I just found out she has cancer. And, she's known about it and hasn't told anyone. I just found out from her doctor."

Ramon loved his mother, but he always had a little anger toward her for not being there for him and his sister. He felt abandoned when she never wrote him when he did time in prison.

"I'll book a flight at my earliest convenience. But, I'm going to have to call you back sis. I'm kind of busy right now."

Minutes later, Ramon pulled into Nisha's apartment. Nisha model walked to the truck. It was her day and she dressed like she knew it. She wore an all her pumps by Prada and her Ray Ban glasses slightly covered her professionally applied make-up. Getting out of the truck, Ramon opened the door for her and gave her a hot pink blindfold.

"Is it on good?" he asked.

"Yes, Daddy," she said, giggling.

Minutes passed and Ramon pulled into a plaza.

"Keep it on, no peeking," Ramon joked.

Nisha smiled. "We must be there. I can feel the truck slowing down."

"We are," Ramon said, stopping the truck and parking it.

Ramon helped Nisha down from the truck and guided her to where he needed her to be.

Nisha stood with all of her teeth showing. "Can I take it off now?"

"Not yet." Ramon turned her toward the building. He wanted her in a good position. "Okay, now you can take it off."

She removed the blindfold and heard a crowd yell, "Happy Birthday!"

Nisha covered her mouth with her hands. She was shocked as she stared at the sign in front of the building that read, 'Pretty Diva's Hair and Nails.'

Nisha's eyes started to tear up, she asked, turning to Ramon. "Is this mine?"

"Only if you want it," Ramon replied.

Nisha jumped into his arms and kissed him all over his face.

"I love you, Ramon," Nisha said.

Ramon was shocked that she used the L-word.

"Just don't point any more guns at me, Nisha, and you know I love you too."

Everyone approached her and gave her hugs and kisses.

Ramon grabbed her hands and said, "Let's go take a look around, sexy."

Nisha walked around the salon, took pictures and sent them to Bree's phone. A cake was brought out, as everyone sang Happy Birthday. Nisha cut Ramon a slice, which he promptly devoured.

As the celebration started to end, everyone made their way to the parking lot. Ramon glanced at his watch. It was close to nine, when shots rang through the air, sending everyone running for cover. Ramon grabbed Nisha, covering her until they reached the truck. He opened the door and pushed her inside.

"What the fuck?" she asked. "Did we lock the salon's door?"

Ramon paused, then made a dash to the front door. He fumbled with the keys, locked the door, then ran back through the parking lot.

"You good, bro?" Charles asked, cutting him off.

"Yeah, meet us at the warehouse," Ramon said.

He burst into a sprint as he heard bullets flying past his head, ricocheting off of the asphalt, and bouncing off of cars. As Ramon ran to the truck, he witnessed Nisha standing on the runner firing shots in the opposite direction. Ramon hopped in the truck, slammed it in drive and pulled off as Nisha got in.

"Ramon, that motherfucker was shooting at you." Nisha said.

"Who?" he asked.

"Somebody in a black hoodie wearing a mask," she said, putting on her seatbelt.

"For real."

"Yes, and I think I grazed him or her because they stop shooting, grabbed their arm, and took off."

Ramon ran two lights. He looked over at Nisha, and saw that she was shaking. He assumed it was her first time using her weapon. He put his hands into hers to calm her down.

Ten minutes later, the warehouse was filled with half of his team.

"What the hell was that?" Vonshee asked.

"That was the end of my birthday." Nisha frowned.

"It's going to be okay," Vonshee replied.

Everyone jumped when J-Dub's phone went off. He took it out of his pocket and looked at it. He slowly lifted his head and looked at Nisha.

"What is it, Jay?" Nisha asked.

He passed the phone to Nisha as Ramon walked over. They both looked at the text, while Nisha read it out loud, "Tell that bitch, I missed this time but next time, I wont. Happy Birthday."

"Are you kidding me?" Vonshee said.

Nisha looked at the sender's number. It was the same number that texted her. "This motherfucker was shooting at me?"

"What did it look like, the aim?" Ramon asked.

Nisha paused. "Now that I think about it. The aim was a little higher."

The shooting didn't start back up until I stood on the floor runner to look for, Ramon."

"Happy Birthday?" Vonshee asked. "You think it's Bree?"

"It sure as hell looks like it." Nisha said.

The mysteries to all the events linked and it took a toll on the crew.

Ramon told everyone to head home, be safe, and take the day off.

Before Fantasia walked out, Ramon asked her, "Do you think you can access the camera's footage?"

"Only the salon's. I can see if they caught anything," Fantasia replied.

"I need to know who this person was at this event."

"I'll see what I can dig up," Fantasia said.

*****

Detective Lopez and her partner pulled into the parking lot of the recent shooting. They were greeted by an uniform cop, Officer Raymond. Raymond had only been on the force for four years, but somehow always ended up at big time crime scenes.

"What do we have here, Raymond?" Lopez asked.

"A shooting, one shot and sent to the hospital. Witnesses say a guy with a hoodie just started shooting," Raymond said, flipping through his notes.

"Did anyone see the direction the shooter ran?" Lopez's partner asked.

"I'm sorry, who are you?" Raymond asked.

"*Lo siento.* This is my new partner, Detective Knowles," Lopez responded. "Please treat her with the same respect as you do me."

The officer stared Knowles down, then continued. "No, no one said they seen where he ran to. But, another witness said there were two people shooting and he said it was a Black woman or maybe Latina standing on a truck."

"Where's the victim?" Knowles asked.

"At Southwest Memorial Hospital. Detective Black is on his way to ask him questions." Raymond said, closing his notepad.

Lopez and Knowles turned to each other. "How the hell did he beat. us here?" Lopez asked.

Knowles walked around the taped off scene. She picked up a shell casting with her pen.

"Hydro Shock," she said as she dropped the shell into a plastic bag. Looking up, she read the sign of a business she's never seen before. "Pretty Diva's. I might have to come by and check this salon out."

"Let's go," Lopez said, walking up.

"Where are we going?" Knowles asked, picking up another shell and getting into their vehicle.

"To the hospital to visit the victim."

A beautiful woman sat at the information desk.

"Excuse me miss," Lopez interrupted the blonde, flashing her badge.

"Oh yes, Detective. How can I help you?" the woman asked.

"I'm here to question a victim who was shot and brought here about an hour ago, Mr. Bridgez."

"Yes ma'am. He's in the emergency room."

"Thank you," Lopez said, tapping Knowles on the shoulder to follow her. Mr. Bridgez told them when he came out of the dollar store, he wanted a Big Bang Burrito from the Mexican Food Truck across the street. As he crossed the street, he noticed someone in a black hoodie wearing a mask, but thought nothing of it."

"Can you give a physical description?" Knowles asked.

Mr. Bridgez paused. "Hmmm, about five eight. It was kind of far."

"What about race?" Lopez asked.

"From what I could see. I think he was black."

"Could you tell if it was a female or male?"

"I would have to say, maybe a female."

"Thanks for your time," Lopez said, handing him a card. "Call me if you can remember anything else."

"All I remember is that I got shot."

An hour later, Lopez and Knowles were back at the Hall.

"So what do you make of all of this?" Lopez asked Knowles.

"I don't know what to think." Knowles answered.

"Well, partner, I would say it's envy or jealousy especially when it's involving two women. I can almost bet you, our other shooter will be a female."

Knowles nodded in agreement.

77

As they left the unmarked vehicle, they passed Detective Black. Black was disliked by most of his peers. Throughout the police force, he was known as a crooked cop and even classified as a snitch. He had fifteen cases on the force and was investigated by the Internal Affairs multiple times. Every time he always managed to slither away like the snake he was. Rumors were Black was a paid member of D-Pop and Facts' drug cartel. But no one has ever had strong enough evidence to link them.

"How are you, ladies?" Black said, walking by.

Neither one answered.

Captain Elder met Lopez and Knowles at the door

"Chief wants to speak to both of you in her office."

They looked at him and walked into the Chief's office.

"Where have you two been?" Chief Taylor asked.

"There was a shooting at Braeswood Plaza," Lopez said.

"We stopped by to check it out."

"Well, I'm putting Black and Styles on that case. I need you two to focus on the grow house. A tip came in, while you were doing God knows what. The caller left a call back number. Her info is on your desk, Lopez."

Lopez called the number and a woman with a Jamaican accent answered. "Yes, hello, I'm Detective Lopez with the HPD. I'm doing a follow up on a case and was given your number to call."

"Yes, I stay three houses down from the house that burnt down some weeks back."

"Okay," Lopez said with a surprise.

"What's your name if you don't mind me asking?"

"I'm Ms. Rahati. I've lived here for seven years and I've seen all type of people go in and out of that house. Multiple cars come and go. I first thought it was just a big family. They would always stay to themselves. I believe the owner of the house died a year and a half ago."

"From what we've learned, that's correct."

"Well, I have a nephew who stayed with me around that time. He started spending time with the men there. My nephew started going over there a lot. He began coming home with a lot of money, he moved out a few months later but he still comes by from time to time to take us out to eat."

"Since the news revealed it was a weed house. Do you think he was selling them?"

"I think so." Ms. Rahati replied. "He always talked about a guy named Cory and one named Maine. He recently got in contact with his brother and father. Now, I barely see him."

"What's your nephew's name? I just want to ask him questions. He is not in any trouble. I just want to talk," Lopez said.

"His name is Rasheem Rahati."

"You talked about his father. What happened to his mother?"

"She's my sister, dead young from breast cancer a year ago."

"I'm sorry to hear that." Lopez said with empathy.

After hanging up, Lopez was exhausted. She wanted to head home. She left, passing her partner's desk.

"You're gone?" Knowles asked.

"Yeah, I'm beat, *Mami*," Lopez answered.

"Well, get some rest. We'll pick up early tomorrow."

"What about you? You don't sleep?" Lopez joked.

"I have a little bit of more paperwork to finish," Knowles said, "Enjoy the rest of your night."

*****

Detective Knowles turned around to her computer after her partner left. She googled Pretty Diva's Hair and Nails. There was nothing. Knowles grabbed her laptop, Gucci bag, car keys and left after her paperwork. On her way down the elevator, she set a reminder on her phone to stop by the new hair salon on her next day off.

CHAPTER 10 – BOND MONEY

Ramon stared out his bedroom window. He turned around and admired his beautiful half-naked girlfriend, laying in bed.

His phone rang and he rushed to answer it, hoping it didn't wake Nisha. "Hello," he answered.

"Good morning, Ramon," Fantasia said. "I pulled up the salon cameras.

From the view of the salon you can only see the parking lot. You can't see the sides so I can't really say if the shooter was there or showed up. It also picked up the whole investigation from HPD, later that night.

"Can you tell it's Nisha in the video?"

"Not really?"

"That's good, right?" Ramon asked.

"Yes and no. I'm only saying that because of the technology that's out these days."

"Okay. How was the first day at the salon?"

"Actually, the first day was good. Nisha might have to keep her weed business and her salon away from each other," Fantasia said.

"Agreed, so how did the shooter know it was Nisha's Birthday?"

Fantasia paused. "I've been wondering the same thing. I can only say this—"

Cutting her off, he said, "There's a mole in the crew."

"'Yes, as you know envy and jealousy is a motherfucker," she added.

"Well, keep me updated and keep digging. I want you to hook up the warehouse with everything also. I want cameras, voice recorders, mics, the whole shabang."

"Now you're speaking my language, Ramon," Fantasia said.

"Great, call me later."

Ramon ended the call, turned and looked at Nisha, she was sitting up in bed. He was about to speak, when Nisha cut him off.

"I know, I heard everything already."

"Well, what do you want for breakfast?" he asked, smiling as reached under the sheets.

******

Detective Knowles walked out of Pretty Diva's with a new hair doo. She had a Brazilian Blowout, with a press and curls added for extra bounce. She felt like a new woman. She also felt like going out. Her detective instincts told her to ask questions about the parking lot shooting. But she didn't want to ruin her first time experience at her new favorite salon with talk. As she hopped into her SUV, her phone rang. "Hello," she answered, cranking up her Aviator.

"How's the off day?" Lopez asked.

"It's fine. I just left the salon," Knowles said, running her fingers through her hair.

"That's great, ballistics just came back. I had them rush the results. One of the shells you collected is from a Glock. The Hydro Shock casing you found has the same markings on it as the one from Cory Beaudruex's murder."

"That name is so familiar. Isn't that the grow house owner?"

"*Correcto, Mami.*" Lopez said in a Spanish accent.

"I wonder what the connection is?"

"I don't know, but enjoy your off day. We'll find out when you return. I need to inform the Chief," Lopez said as she hung up.

*****

Rasheem entered the High Times Smoke Shop surprised, when he seen Vonshee. He always had a crush on her. But never asked her out, knowing she and Charles were in a relationship. He picked up a few items and walked to the cashier's desk. Vonshee lift her head from her station, doing a double take. "What are you doing on this side of town? she asked, smiling.

"Actually, I just came in to get a few things. I didn't know you worked here," he said. "Why are you working here? Don't you make all that money with Nisha?"

Vonshee giggled. "Well, some of our best clients came from right here."

Tilting his head. "Really?" Rasheem asked.

"Yup." Vonshee answered, ringing his items up.

It was the first time Rasheem had seen her by herself. She stood five feet four, caramel skin, with long black hair and hips to die for. Plus, her nails were always on point with a jazzy look.

"Want to go out on a date."

Not showing one bit of flatteries, she took a breath. "I'm sorry Rasheem but, you know I'm committed to Charles. If it was a different situation, I would've said yes. Besides, with those scratches on your neck, it looks like you're enjoying the single life."

"These aren't what you think," he claimed.

Rasheem paid the bill, smiled and left out. He took out his phone from his pocket and started texting. He noticed Vonshee, eyeing him until he finally exited out of the parking lot. Rasheem made his way back to the warehouse. The organization had taken a big hit when the first grow house burned down. But, J-Dub, Charles, and Rasheem had other plans to make up for the lost funds. They started running coke without anyone knowing. They knew Ramon wouldn't have approved of the move, scoring from Facts, the coke connection. But this was a plan to make millions way faster than Ramon's weed business.

Rasheem walked in and asked, "So we're using Ramon's warehouse to sell coke behind his back, and he's basically head over hill-over this bitch?"

"Look, man, we got to where we are because of him and Cory. I can't just let you disrespect them like that," Charles said.

"Sometimes you have to start from the bottom. Then once you reach the top of the throne, then you chop off heads. Destroy your enemies completely."
J-Dub said, smirking.

"Who's the enemy?" Charles asked, squinting at J-Dub.

"Shit! Life," J-Dub answered. "Who else?"

"Sounds like some 48 Laws of Power shit," Rasheem laughed.

"Sounds like you're both on some bullshit," Charles said as he put two bricks of coke in a bag.

"Just sit back and enjoy the success, Rasheem. We're going to be big. And we gonna be running this town," J-Dub said.

"I agree." Charles nodded. "Now, help me put this in my stash spot."

After they hid the coke in Charles's car, Rasheem asked, even though he had no intentions of going. "You want me to ride with you?"

"Naw, I'm good," Charles answered, getting into his Lexus. "I'll call when I'm on my way back."

"That's a bad ass car." Rasheem said as Charles pulled off into the street.

"You can get something better than that if you stick with me, lil bro." J-Dub said with a devious smile. "Follow me, I need you to do me a favor. You might even like this yourself."

"Oh shit, this gotta be good," Rasheem said, rubbing his hands together.

*****

Ramon received a call from his sister. She told him their mother's condition was worse. He had forgotten to book the flight because of the shooting. His sister told him don't worry about, she booked him a flight for Sunday. Ramon agreed to the date and time. He loved his sister. If she requested his presence, he was on his way. Nisha loved that about him.

Ramon watched Nisha brush her teeth as her phone rang. She put the phone on speaker. "Hello."

"Hey, beautiful," Vonshee said.

"Look, I wanted to do an all girls night out. I don't like how your birthday ended."

"Ramon has to leave on Sunday for Cali. I want to spend time with him," Nisha said after spitting toothpaste into the sink and wiping her lips.

"Well, bring him. You know what, fuck it. Let's invite everybody."

"We can do that, but you have to call everyone."

Vonshee chuckled. "I will. We might even see Bree."

"Yeah, I doubt it," Nisha said.

"Anyways, I'll call you in a bit. Customers just walked in," Vonshee said.

After hanging up with Vonshee, Nisha jumped when Ramon said.

"So, you're inviting me to an all girl's night out?"

Nisha giggled. "Nope."

"I'm just joking. I'll be there. I'm going to go by the warehouse house. You want to roll with me?" he asked, pointing to his Coogi shirt.

"No, I have to do some drops. But, I'll see you at D-Live tonight."

"Bet." he said and kissed her. "Damn, your breath's minty."

"It's Crest," she said, grabbing his crotch.

"Don't start nothing you can't finish and don't forget to lock up," he said, grabbing her ass.

*****

Charles answered Vonshee's call via bluetooth. "What's up, V?'"

"Where you at, Big Head?" she laughed.

"I'm in Acre Homes, doing a quick drop."

"Are you coming by to see me today?"

"Yeah, I got you."

"Your homie Rasheem is a little weird," Vonshee said, smacking her lips.

"First, that's not my homie. Second, why do you even say he's weird?"

"He came by here today, tripping. He even asked me out on a date."

Charles laughed.

"What's so funny? He's a kid. I had to let him down easy."

"Well, I think he has a crush on you."

Vonshee chuckled. "I think he wants to take your spot."

"Quit it," Charles said as he noticed a police car in his mirror. "Let me call you right back, babe."

Charles hung up quickly and sat up in the drivers seat. The cop's sirens and lights came on. Charles slowly pulled over, not really caring. He knew were he had his stash spot, and all of his papers were good. He rolled down his window as the officer walked up. "Is there a problem officer?"

"License and registration," the officer asked.

"Is there a problem?" Charles asked again.

"Yes, I'm an officer of the law and I'm asking for your info. And, you're not complying."

Charles reached and grabbed the items from his glove compartment, and handed them to the officer.

"Sit still until I return," the officer said as he walked back to his car slowly.

Moments later, Charles noticed an unmarked pulling up behind the officer's car. A tall black man in a suit joined the officer in the squad car. The black man got out and walked to Charles's window.

Charles asked a third time. "Is there a problem, officer?"

The man tilted his head. "Maybe you should try Detective Black."

"Detective?"

"Yup, I'm going to need you to step out of the vehicle. Then, I need you to join my buddy over there," Black said, pointing at the uniform officer.

Charles mumbled, but complied.

"Nice car, any weapons hidden in it?"

Charles said nothing as he walked off with the cop.

"What's he doing?" Charles asked, while the officer searched him.

"He's searching your vehicle for narcotics and anything else you might have in your car."

Charles made a mental note that the name of the detective was Black. He looked at the officer's badge and name tag. He seen it said Clarks engraved in it. He eyed Black and seen him answer his phone, then lower his head.

Moments later, Black emerged from the car, holding a kilo of the purest cocaine in the city.

Black smiled. "Cuff his ass."

Charles dropped his head as the officer slapped the cuffs on. It would be his second time going to jail for narcotics.

*****

Nisha was back doing her drops when an ideal crossed her mind when she drove by her apartment. She didn't want her salon and her weed business mixing with each other so she decided to turn her spot into a trap house and move in with Ramon. Her apartment was in the back, which meant people wouldn't see the customer traffic.

Later that night, Nisha stared at her curves in her mirror. She was ready to party. Growing up in foster care and in the streets with her brother helped push fear from her mind. She was determined not to hide because some jealous person wanted her spot. She arrived at D-Live in her Christian Dior pink dress. All eyes were on her as she skipped the line and went in.

Henroe hugged her and pointed to the VIP, where her friends were. Ramon stood at the bar talking to people she had never seen before.

Nisha walked up to him as "All Eyes On Me" by The Game featuring Jermiah played in the background. Nisha grabbed his hand, pulling him away from his conversation. "Dance with me, Daddy. You can talk to them later." They made it to the dance floor. Nisha twerked and danced all over him. Feeling his manhood rocking up, she bent over and pushed her ass against him, turned around, then grabbed him. "You're mine tonight," she whispered, biting his ear.

"Y'all look like y'all was having fun," Fantasia said as Nisha and Ramon turned back to the section.

"We were," Nisha giggled.

Fantasia excused herself and left VIP, heading to the Ladies Room.

*****

Fantasia fixed her make-up in the mirror, noticing a beautiful woman staring at her. Fantasia thought she looked like one of the women that was there at the house fire. It was her. "Has anyone ever told you that you look just like that singer, Fantasia?" the woman asked.

"Yes, all the time," Fantasia answered. "You should see my friend. She thinks she looks like Beyoncé."

"Well, you know what they say, 'All black folks look alike.'" the woman said, whipping her make-up off.

"Yup,"

"Funny thing is, my last name is Knowles, no relations, sad to say," the woman laughed.

"Well, you're still good aren't you?"

"Wish I knew how to sing. I would've chosen a different career."

Fantasia couldn't resist. "What do you do?"

Knowles slurred. "Law enforcement, ewww."

Fantasia smiled into the mirror. "I'm into tech."

"Well, at least you seem like you love it."

"Likewise. Do you need me to get you an Uber?" Fantasia asked.

"No, I'm good. I can manage. It was nice meeting you," Knowles said then exited the restroom.

Fantasia waited then went back to her crew.

"Damn girl, you've been gone a long time. You okay?" Vonshee asked.

"I just ran into one of the officers that was at the grow house fire. I do not forget faces. I know it was her and she told me she was in law enforcement, and she said her last name was Knowles," Fantasia said, raising her eyebrow.

"We need to leave, right now," Rasheem said.

"Naw, she was tipsy. I think she was leaving," Fantasia said.

Ramon's phone rang. He pulled it out of his 501's and answered.

"What?" he said after listening for a minute.

Nisha glanced at Ramon, looking worried.

After he hung up, Nisha asked, "Boo, who was that?"

"That was Charles. He said he got popped with a kilo of coke," Ramon said, staring at Vonshee.

"What the fuck?" Vonshee yelled, causing people to look over. "That's why his phone's been going to voicemail?"

"Why the hell did he have a kilo?" Nisha asked.

"I don't know, but we might have to do what Rasheem said and leave right now. I got to go get his bond money," Ramon said as the rest of the crew left.

CHAPTER 11 – THE PICK UP

Hours later, Charles had climbed into the back seat of Ramon's Denali. Vonshee swung at him as he tried to close his door.

"Charles, what the hell is wrong with you?" Vonshee yelled.

Ramon and Nisha laughed.

As Ramon pulled away from the jail, he asked with a serious tone. "Now, for real. How the hell you get caught with kilo of cocaine?"

While Charles stared out the window, Vonshee smacked him in the back of the head, "Are you going to answer us or not?"

Charles took a deep breath. "Look! I just wanted to make a little extra money. J-Dub and I started dealing coke on the regular. We knew y'all wouldn't approve, so we started selling behind y'all backs."

Nisha turned around from the front seat and asked, "Are you serious?"

"Hold up, Nisha," Vonshee said.

"Let me ask his dumb ass. Are you serious? Look at all the shit we got going on."

"Look, the money was good," Charles said.

"All money ain't good money, bro. We do good growing our own weed and we have multiple strands that we put our own price on. Why the hell would you want to deal with coke? You know we are already making good money."

Charles huffed. "Yeah, I know, but we took a big hit and I just wanted to make some extra money."

"True," Ramon began, "but you have to let me worry about that. And as long as we're all eating right, that's the only thing that matters to me."

"You right," Charles said, dropping his head.

Ramon sighed. "Look this ain't no regular urban story where we have to sell five hundred kilos to be considered successful. I have a dispensary, a label, plus my own crew that I love. Trust me when I say we're good, bro."

"Plus, we don't need any extra heat on us," Nisha said.

"Boy, you owe us $5,000. Your bond was fifty bands," Vonshee said, smacking him in the back of his head again.

"I'll pay everyone when we make it to my condo," Charles said.

"What happened?" Nisha asked.

Charles paused for a moment. "The shit was kind of weird. I got pulled over and it was like they knew exactly where the stash was. I watched the detective answer his phone. Then, he jumped out with the coke. I had already did some deliveries earlier."

"Detectives?" Nisha asked.

Ramon made a right down Richmond. "I think you were selling to an undercover."

"Could have," Charles replied.

"I think you were set up," Nisha said, applying her lipstick. "That's what it sounds like to me."

"What do we do now?" Vonshee asked.

"Shit, now we get him the best lawyer in Houston," Ramon said as he made a left turn into Charles's condo driveway.

After dropping Charles and Vonshee off, Ramon turned to Nisha. "Want to catch a movie? It's still early and we're close to AMC 30."

Nisha eyed the movie theater and agreed on a movie.

"Cool," Ramon said. "But first, we smoke. I'm going to swing by the gas station to get some cigars and you're rolling."

Nisha laughed. "Why do you want me to roll up?"

"Because you have the best rolling skills I've ever seen."

CHAPTER 12 – GEEK SQUAD

Fantasia had spent Sunday morning in front of her screen after Ramon left for Cali. Her hacking skills enabled her to uncover crucial information and get into what was suppose to be special systems and networks. She found out DetectiveKnowles's last name from their encounter. She searched Facebook, Instagram, Twitter, TikTok, and just about any other social media page that was linked to her. She discovered Knowles's first name and discovered she and Nisha attended the same school at the same time. Fantasia was proud that her hacking training paid off. Steven Free, a co-worker and ex she met while working for Geek Squad taught her how to hack. Fantasia became one of the best hackers in the state and had no knowledge of it.

Fantasia called Nisha as soon as she was done. "I think you need to get to my house, *rapido*."

"Why?" Nisha asked.

"You'll find out when you get here."

"Well, I'm on my way, soon as I finish this quick transaction," Nisha said, excitedly before hanging up.

Once Nisha arrived. Fantasia told her to have a seat.

Nisha squinted her eyes and took her seat.

"I went digging up some info on our detective. It took me a couple of hours. But, I'm me! Here's what I found out. Miss Knowles is the daughter of Jonathan and Kellie Knowles, no relations to Queen B. Miss Knowles went to Westbury High School in the ninth grade, but her family relocated to Germany because her father was in the military. Kellie divorced him due to his infidelity. After that, she moved back to Houston with her daughter, who studied law and became an officer. She excelled so well and so fast, she became a detective her sixth year on the force. And, that's when she became the youngest member of the Narcotics and Vice Task Force, where she was partnered with Priscilla Lopez, an eleven year vet."

"I'm gonna cut you off. What does this got to do with me?" Nisha asked.

"Didn't you go to Westbury?"

"Yeah, so?"

"I pulled up your year book," Fantasia said, turning the screen to Nisha. "Do you know this person?" she asked, pointing at the photo.

Nisha glanced at the picture. "Oh My God...That's me, Rosa, Vonshee, Bree and Simeerah," Nisha said. "Knowles was Simeerah's last name?"

"I'm guessing but, this is who I met in the restroom at the club."

"Are you serious?" Nisha asked. "She started a group called the Pretty Diva Clique. Now, she's a cop?"

"Not just any cop, a detective. So, we need to do something fast. She and her partner is over the grow house case and they both were at the shooting. The salon's cameras picked up everything that night."

"Well, we moved the operation, so we should be good, right?"

"Yes, for the time being," Fantasia said optimistically.

*****

Vonshee was serving a customer when Rasheem walked into the smoke shop.

"This must be your favor spot, now?" Vonshee asked, approaching her cashier desk.

"You sell handcuffs here?" Rasheem asked.

"Huh, yeah," Vonshee said, looking at him with a smirk. "You kinky?"

"Naw, I need them for a project," he replied.

"Yeah, okay," Vonshee giggled, going around the other counter to grab the handcuffs.

Rasheem paid for the cuffs and stared at Vonshee.

"What?" Vonshee asked, trying not to frown.

"Nothing, I'll see you later."

"Rasheem, are you okay? You haven't been yourself lately."

"Yeah, I'm good," he said as he walked out the shop.

After Rasheem walked out, Vonshee phoned Nisha.

"Hello," Nisha asked.

Nisha, this nigga Rasheem came in here tripping."

"Girl, what do you mean?" Nisha Laughed.

"He came in here asking for some handcuffs, looking at me all weird and shit. Then he said he'll see me later."

"He just likes you, Vonshee. Maybe a little to much. But, you wanna hear something even more bizarre than that?"

"What?" Vonshee asked sounding frustration.

"The cop Fantasia said she seen at the grow house fire and the club, guess who is she is?"

"I don't know, just tell me."

"Simeerah."

"Simeerah? Not ringing a bell." Vonshee said, clearing her throat.

"Pretty Diva Clique Simeerah from high school."

"What!?" Are you serious, Nisha?"

"I'm dead serious. She became a cop." Nisha said. "And, she's over the grow house case."

Vonshee was wowed. "I can't believe it."

"I know, so I think that trumps your Rasheem loverboy story. Call me when you get off. I'm about to stop by Bree's mom's house."

*****

Nisha pulled into the driveway of the Third Ward home of Mrs. Barrett. She knocked on the door and was met by a beautiful older woman.

"Nisha, what are you doing on this side of town?" Mrs. Barrett asked jokingly.

"Hello. Mrs. Barrett. I was wondering if I could speak with you for a minute, if you don't mind."

"Yes, come on in, baby," Mrs. Barrett said, opening the screen door.

Nisha stepped in. "Have you seen or heard from your daughter Breonna?"

"No, I haven't heard from her in about seven or eight months."

"Are you serious?" Nisha asked.

"Yes, I didn't really agree with how she was bringing in money. She was dancing, we had a fight and I haven't seen her since. Why are you asking such a question like that?"

"Well, we haven't seen or heard from her in about two to three months," Nisha said, wiping her eyes.

"Awww, poor baby. My daughter has always been known to pull disappearing acts for several months. She's just like her father," Mrs. Barrett said, extending her arms to give Nisha an embracing hug.

"Yeah, but I miss her and so much has happened since she left."

"Bree always does things like this. She goes missing for some time then she'll return when she run out of money," Mrs. Barrett said. "However, I do know that her phone bill was just paid."

"It was?" Nisha asked confused.

"Yes, she's on my family plan. Her phone's bill was paid last week."

"So, she's okay. But, why hasn't she called or answered my texts?"

Mrs. Barrett smiled. "All I can tell you is this. Bree is complicated. When shit not going her way, she runs away. She'll be back. Trust me. A mother knows."

"Well, Mrs. Barrett, I have to go. Can you please text or call me if you hear from her."

"Oh, sure, baby girl. I'll call you."

Nisha headed down 288 back to the southwest side of Houston. Mrs. Barrett's positive attitude gave Nisha a little hope about her friend. Everyone thought Bree was the shooter from the salon. And, the words from Cory's wife Karla kept echoing in her head envy and jealousy is always around you.

Nisha yielded to the right and got on Highway 59 before deciding to visit Vonshee at the smoke shop.

*****

Detective Lopez and Detective Knowles were sitting in the Chief's office when she entered. "How are you ladies doing this morning?"

"We're doing good, Chief."

The Chief held up her hand, cutting Lopez off. She took a sip of her French Cappuccino, then motioned Lopez to continue.

"As I was saying, I understand you gave the parking lot case to Black and Smith. But these cases are linked and I want to work both of them."

"How are both of these cases linked?" the Chief asked.

"Well, the bullets from the parking lot and the bullet from Cory Beaudruex's murder are a match."

"Which means whoever was doing the shooting in the parking lot had something to do with the grow house owner's murder," the Chief said, taking another sip of her cappuccino.

"Yes," Knowles answered.

The Chief dropped her glasses. "How about this, Lopez. Your primary case is the burned grow house. Black and Smith stays on the case as lead but you are more then welcome to assist on the parking lot shooting, but only on your free time. Any new info or intel comes straight to me."

"Thanks, Chief," Lopez said, tapping Knowles to leave.

After making it back to their desks, Lopez called Knowles over. "Check this out. I had one of my informants do a stake out on that growth house. He claimed he bought from them before. He said two women came by to do an estimate of the house. But I found out there was no insurance linked to it. Got a partial plate number, tracked the car down, found out it belongs to a Lori Johnson."

"Well, that's good, right?" Knowles asked.

"Yes, and I got a driver's license photo of the owner." Lopez said as she pointed at the screen.

Knowles did a double take after spinning around in her chair. "Wait a minute, I know her."

"For real?" Lopez asked. "Well, we need to speak with her, we have some questions. And. guess what? I have a an address. The Detectives arrived at the address on Fantasia's ID. They knocked on the door and were met by an older woman with nice features."

"Yes, can I help you?" the woman asked.

"Yes, ma'am, I'm Detective Lopez and this is my partner Detective Knowles. We're here to speak to Ms. Lori Johnson. Are you her mother?"

"Yes, I'm Mrs. Johnson."

"Well, we'd like to speak with her about an arson," Knowles said.

Mrs. Johnson laughed. "I don't think you're looking for the right Lori."

"How could you be so sure?" Lopez questioned.

"My daughter is a MIT Grad. She loves working with computers. She's practically a nerd, a computer geek. She always said she was going to work for a big company. She left Geek Squad to work for one. Why would she be involved with an arson?"

"Do you know the name of the company?" Lopez asked.

"I think she said it's called Corporate G Enterprise. Some kind of tech company. I remember she said they did well in finding new and faster ways to deliver products. If I can remember correctly I think she said her boss's name was Mr. Maine."

Lopez, and Knowles turned and eyed each other. "Do you know if she's involved in anything illegal?" Knowles asked.

Mrs. Johnson frowned. "Like I said, she's a MIT Grad."

"Okay, okay, ma'am," Lopez said, putting her hands up. "If she happens to stop by, can you give her my card. We need to speak with her."

Mrs. Johnson faked a smile. "Will do."

Back in the unmarked, Lopez looked at her notepad. "So, we've interviewed two people and both said their family members works for someone named Maine. And, what the hell is Corporate G Enterprise?"

"I just checked the Better Business Bureau and there's nothing in their database registered with that name," Knowles said, tapping at her phone's screen.

"That must be the name of Mr. Maine's operation. Rasheem Rahati must be a runner and Ms. Johnson must be his tech girl. Looks like everything is coming together," Lopez said, putting the car in drive and speeding off.

*****

Charles was at his lawyer's office discussing all the details on his cases. Jimmy Chaney had earned the title as the best criminal defense lawyer in the city. Mr. Chaney listened as Charles explained everything that happened that evening. From the moment the uniform pulled him over to Detective Black showing up on the scene.

"You're being charged with Procession of a Controlled Substance up to a thousand grams, with the intent to deliver," Chaney said.

"I know, " Charles said then turned toward Vonshee.

"Please believe me, I understand that people do different things to get money, including selling drugs. I will try to do my best to get you the best outcome for this case. I promise you will get your money's worth."

They shook hands, then Charles and Vonshee left Chaney's office.

Once they reached Charles's car he phoned Ramon.

"What's up?" Ramon answered.

"I just left the lawyer's office. He said he's going to help me."

"That's cool. I told you he was the best."

"I understand what you were trying to say in the truck," Charles said.

"I hope so, bro. It took us years to get here, you can't just rush success. You have to take it slow, plan it, then execute it."

"I know," Charles said. "But, anyways. How's your mom?"

"Cancer, you know that shit a motherfucker."

"You'll be good. Y'all just keep y'all heads up."

"Thanks fam, but I gotta go. Stay away from that coke shit. Tell J-Dub he tripping too."

After Charles dropped off Vonshee, he stopped by the warehouse, where J-Dub was standing outside smoking a Newport cigarette.

"What kind of bird don't fly?" J-Dub asked, smiling.

Never hearing the phrase before, Charles asked. "What kind?"

"A jail bird," J-Dub laughed.

Charles stared, not thinking the joke was one bit funny.

"So are you gonna keep selling or not?" J-Dub asked, putting his arm around Charles.

"Man, I really don't know," Charles said, removing J-Dub's arm.

"Look, whoever you sold to, was dirty. Just don't sell them shit no more, Especially if you haven't known them that long. People become confidential snitches these days to save their own asses." J-Dub said as they walked into the warehouse office.

"Naw, I already know."

J-Dub frowned. "Just be a little more careful next time. We gotta get this money."

Rasheem stuck his head in. "I'm about to go," he said.

Charles looked at Rasheem and nodded. "What's up, Rasheem?"

"What's up. Charles. You good with the case and shit?"

"Yeah, I'm good for right now."

When Rasheem strolled off, Charles turned to J-Dub. "That's one weird kid."

J-Dub laughed, showcasing all his golds. "Naw, trust me, he's loyal to a fault. He's just young."

"Well, loyalty gets you far these days."

"True. I was loyal to Cory all the way to his grave. We were close. Ramon came in the picture a little later, then he brung you in. Everyone loved Cory. Some people even feared him. I saw him go from nothing to something, quick. Ramon gave him that growing your own weed shit and Cory took off."

"For real?" Charles asked.

"Hell yeah. I left to the army, dishonorable discharge, came back two years later, and both of them were millionaires. I was amazed at it." J-Dub said.

"We could build our own empire and be where Ramon's at."

"I don't know, Jay."

"You like money, right?"

"Yeah, duh," Charles said. "Who don't?"

J-Dub smiled. "Well, ride and I'll guide us to the road of success. Everything here is in the works. You just have to be patient."

"I think we've been patient, that's the problem. It's time to go out there and really go get it"

"Agreed, but ride with me and we'll take this thing over the right way."

CHAPTER 13 - THE BAD GUY

Later Vonshee and Nisha visited Fantasia. When they arrived, Fantasia opened the door and ran back to her computer. The skills Fantasia acquired always came in handy. She turned from her desk. "Okay, Pretty Divas, I have good news."

"You do?" Vonshee asked.

"Yes, I did a little tracking and hacking. I found out that Bee's phone goes to an industrial area in Fifth Ward. I tried the Find My Phone app on it. It goes to the same spot every night. But. I can only get a ratio on the ping due to all the security and buildings. I'll try to do more and find out more."

"It's okay, Fanny," Nisha said.

"She'll turn up soon." Fantasia assuredly said.

"I hope so," Vonshee said.

Nisha clapped her hands. "So, today I had an epiphany. We've almost made $222,000 together in a short amount of time. When Ramon gave me the salon for my birthday. I decided I wanted to go big. I want Pretty Divas to be a brand. I want us into hair, cosmetics, jewelry, books, and even health care. I've even considered real-estate. I want us to be internationally known."

"How are we supposed to do this?" Vonshee asked, raising an eyebrow.

"Well, help me steer the money into the right investments. We need an exit plan."

Fantasia raised her finger. "I can help with that."

"Good," Nisha said. "Because I want to be big like the Rockefellers, the Kochs, the Morgans, the Waltons, and maybe even the Trumps. I want me and Ramon to be like Jay and Beyoncé. They're both rich and humble."

"I like this mindset." Vonshee said.

"Me too," Fantasia said. "But where is all this coming from?"

"I've been on Youtube," Nisha said, "Did you know that slave masters already showed us wealth and really how to get it. But us blacks and latinos help them become wealthier. First we buy all their products. You know their electric luxury cars, clothes, diamonds, gold and we even call ourselves investing our hard earned money into their stocks. I've figured out we lack knowledge. We put money into these peoples hands and these are the same ones who raped our ancestors. We really know nothing about the U.S. Banking Systems. But, we can tell you when some new Jay's come out or when that new Drake album about to drop."

Vonshee and Fantasia turned to each other wide eyed.

"I want us to reach three million in a year. I think we can do it . Ramon, he's making almost four million a year. We're the Pretty Divas and I think we can make that also, if we really put our minds to it."

"I agree with you, Nisha," Vonshee said.

"You know what? I agree with you too, girl. Let's do it." Fantasia said.

Vonshee smile. "And FYI, that new Drake album go hard."

*****

Detective Lopez and Knowles searched through all sorts of files and paperwork linked to a guy named Maine. Knowles searched the web and cross referenced the name in the criminal database.

Seconds later, Knowles stared at a picture not sure if she recognized the sole on the screen or not.

"Look at this, Lopez."

Knowles said, pointing at the computer screen.

Lopez looked and read the name loudly. "Ramon Dumas."

"Keep reading," Knowles suggested.

Lopez kept reading and discovered Ramon and Cory went to jail together.

"So they did know each other."

"Yeah," Knowles said, "Mr. Ramon Dumas better known as Maine, and Cory Beaudruex got arrested together. Both did a month in the county."

Lopez scrolled some more and read. "It also says here, they were arrested again together. Cory bonded out. And, Maine went to jail on a four year sentence. He did eighteen months and was released from TDC. He finished his time on the streets."

"Then two years later Cory was shot and killed," Knowles said.

Lopez stepped back, putting her hand on her chin. "You think Ramon killed Cory because he wanted the weed business to himself, or maybe he was mad that he went to prison and Cory didn't."

Knowles leaned back in her chair. "I don't know. But we need to find that gun and find Mr. Dumas."

*****

The next morning, Nisha drove her Impala through the maddening traffic. Henroe, the club manager, called and requested another ten pounds. He had become Nisha's highest. paying customer. The traffic was congested, gridlocked traffic at every stop light. When Nisha finally arrived. Henroe was staring at his watch.

"Yeah, I know," Nisha said, exiting her car.

"Almost thought you bailed out on me."

"I can't miss no money, crazy," she said, grabbing the duffles bags out of her trunk.

"I know that's right. Have you seen Bree?" Henroe asked with concern.

"No, why do you ask?" Nisha asked, squinting her eyes at him.

"Because, I haven't heard from her since she left my house about three months ago."

"What, why was she at your house?"

A smile crept to Henroe's face.

"You know what. Don't answer that," Nisha said, unzipping the duffles.

"Well, I hope she's doing okay," Henroe said, handing Nisha a suitcase of honey. Nisha didn't answer. She was too skeptical about who was trying to gun her down at her birthday celebration. And, so far it looks like her friend Bree was the only answer.

*****

The drug world was taking the city by storm. Most wanted felons were running around. Bloods, Crips, MS13s, the Cartel and just about any known cliques had taken over the streets. Houston Law Enforcements was determined to get things back in order. Detective Black was at his desk when he received a call on his personal phone. It was his Confidential Informant.

"What do you have me?" Black asked.

"So far as I know, Ramon's right hand man is fighting drug charges. You should know that already. His crew is basically being can by his new bitch and a couple of other people. And he hasn't been seen since he left for California about two weeks ago," the informer said.

"What about your partner? Is he doing his part?"

"Yes, let's just say his jealousy will get the best of him."

"Good, I need everything planned right. I need more than just a weed operation bust."

"I'm working on it," the informer replied.

"We'll see. Call me when you have more. And, tell your mother I said, hello."

"Yeah, good luck with that. You're closer to her than I am."

After Black ended his call, he headed out the door. He passed Knowles and asked her if she would join him to go investigate the shooting from the parking lot.

Knowles smiled and said, "I can't, Black, you should take Lopez with you."

Black grinned. "You know me and her don't get along."

"You don't get along with a lot of cops, Black. I wonder why?"

Maybe they don't like the way I do my job."

"Well, you have done some things in the past that'll make people second guess your professionalism."

"Sometimes you have to get dirty. I can promise you, one day you're going to have to make a life changing decision. Your badge and your honor will be put to the test, a test of true loyalty."

"So, what about your badge?"

Black twisted his face. "What about it?"

"You've never dishonored it?" Knowles asked.

"I'll dishonor myself before I dishonor my badge. Unless it's involving my children," Black answered. "What about you?"

Knowles paused. "Well, I haven't been put in a situation like that, yet."

"Exactly," Black said. "If you can't answer now, you'll be the same way whenever the situation does comes."

Knowles stared him down for a moment. "You might be right. But I'm pretty sure I'll do the right thing when the time comes."

CHAPTER 14 – WEB OF LIES

Monday morning traffic was a disaster in Houston. Detective Knowles arrived to work late. She turned on her computer and pulled up her G-Mail. Once logged on, she received an email with an attachment. Thinking it was spam, she moved the cursor to delete it, until she saw the sender's name, Lori Johnson.

"What the hell?" Simeerah said.

She opened the email and clicked on the link. A black screen popped up in the corner of her computer. 'What do you and your partner want with me?' Knowles read.

Knowles typed back, 'I want to talk to you about an arson.'

"I had nothing to do with that," Lori typed back.

"But, you know about it," Knowles typed.

The next response sent shockwaves down Knowles's spinal cord.

"I know about a lot of things. Simeerah Knowles, daughter of Kellie and Jonathan Knowles, parents divorced in 2008 due to your father's infidelities, you and your mother returned back to the states from Germany, you graduated from Clear Lake High School, attended college at TSU, then transferred to Texas Law School. Later you joined the HPD, moved up the ranks, and later became a Detective and partnered with eleven year vet Priscilla Lopez, currently assigned to the Grow House Fire case on West Bellfort. And, your current location is 2111 Austin Street in Downtown Houston. Is that enough?"

Knowles stared at the screen then typed, 'You've done your research?'

"Yes, If you want to talk in person? I'll ping you an address to your phone."

Knowles' phone beeped. She picked her phone up and swiped it. There was a ping from an unknown number with a text that read, "Come alone and leave your phone in your car."

Thirty minutes later, Knowles and Lori were standing face to face.

"Hello, Ms. Johnson," Knowles said.

"What do you wish to know?"

"Where's your boss?"

Lori smirked. "I'm going to suggest you move on to your next question."

"We've linked you, Ramon, Rasheem. and Cory together. Not to mention a grow house that was burned down three months ago. All I want to do is talk to him."

"I don't think he'd agree to meet with you."

Detective Knowles sighed. "We have three cases linked to him and Cory Beaudruex. I really want to eliminate him as murder suspect."

"First, you can't link him to that. Second, you don't have anything on us from the grow house fire. All of your information is circumstantial. And third, we only met each other at the club by accident. I didn't even think cops partied in those types of establishments."

"What can I say, I like the nightlife," Knowles said, smiling.

"If you think Ramon would kill his best friend? Why would he?"

"Money. It's the root to all evil, Ms. Johnson."

"Maybe so, but not in this circle. Loyalty and respect rules over everything here."

Knowles tilted her head. "Is that right?"

"Yes, this crew has been together for a long time. And, Cory and Ramon's friendship was bigger than money. It was about respect. Ramon even took a case for Cory. He did eighteen months because Cory had twins on the way."

Knowles wasn't really shocked. She had just read about the case but, she didn't know the details behind it. "That explains why Cory didn't go to TDC and Ramon did."

"Yes, is there anything else?" Lori asked.

Knowles paused, putting her fingers on her chin. "Yeah, do you have any clue who would want to burn y'all operation down? If so, can you help?"

Lori laughed, amused at the questions. "What operation, Detective? I'll tell my friend that Detective Knowles wants to speak with him. It'll be his decision to speak with you or not. And since I'm not under arrest, I'll only tell you to enjoy the rest of your day. Oh, and one more thing, Detective. If we meet again and I ask you to leave your phone in the car, please follow my request."

Lori smiled and walked away.

Knowles smiled as the super-star look-alike hopped into her vehicle and burned rubber on her way out. Pulling her phone out, Knowles saw her phone go from disable to enable.

"She's good, too good. I think we can use her on the force in our tech department," Knowles said, jumping in her SUV.

*****

Fantasia did several stops, not knowing if Knowles would follow her or not. Later, she made her way to the salon. She also phoned Ramon, who answered on the second ring.

"What's up, Fanny?"

"We have a small problem. I just spoke with a detective and she knows about us and they have you as suspect?"

"What the hell? Why would they suspect me?"

"Don't know. But we can't let this shit get back to Nisha. I just don't want no bullshit getting out of control."

"I'll handle Nisha. Don't bring this up to her. I mean it,"

Fantasia laughed. "Why would I do that? My loyalty is with you first."

"Good, keep me updated. I'll call you later."

After grabbing her purse, Fantasia made her way into the salon, and was approached by one of the salon workers.

"A cop came in here yesterday," the the worker said and paused. "He asked about our cameras."

"What did he want to know about them?"

"He wanted footage involving the July parking lot shooting."

"And, what did you tell him?" Fantasia asked.

"I told him, we don't have footage on that. We just opened the day after so we don't have any footage before that."

"Good work," Fantasia said. "I'll make sure to tell Nisha to give you a nice bonus for your quick thinking."

The worker smiled and rubbed her hands together, like she knew money was involved.

"Now, let's talk about hair because I need my edges done," Fantasia said with a laugh.

*****

Nisha and her friend were heading their separate ways. She received a text from the unknown number again and read it out loud, "The Queen Pin who cheats on the King. How delightful? But did you know most kingdoms fall behind a woman?" Nisha looked up from her phone and scanned the parking lot. She called the number back but only received a Text Me App voicemail. She sent a text that read, 'Why don't you just be a big girl and show yourself.'

The number didn't reply.

"I can't believe this bitch is watching me," she said to herself.

Almost dropping her phone as it rung in her hand, she seen it was Ramon's number.

"Hey, Babe," she answered.

"What's up?"

Nisha took a deep breath. "Nothing much, I'm on my way to the salon."

"Cool, Fantasia is already there."

"Are you doing, okay?" Nisha asked.

"Nisha, this shit is crazy. All this shit seems like it's coming down too fast. I don't know to stop or shut it down for a minute."

"Well, whatever you decide, I'm here to ride with you."

"Thanks, Boo." Ramon said, making a kissing noise through the phone. "You ever thought about moving away and settling down?"

"Yeah, but what about my girls? Plus, I want to know what happened to my brother. That does not sit well with me. It's still an unsolved mystery. I can't just leave like that."

Ramon Laughed. "You sound just like him. Y'all are related."

"I know," Nisha giggled.

"When you and Fantasia get done at the salon, swing by the warehouse and round everyone up and call me."

"Okay, Love you, bye," Nisha said before hanging up.

*****

The warehouse reaped of marijuana as Vonshee walked in, but she never complained about it. A smell she knew meant money.

After Nisha requested that everyone meet her in the office, she called Ramon on speaker phone.

"As you all should know," Ramon began, "The laws are in our company now. I don't like it. It leaves a bad taste in my mouth. I've reconstructed my business due to a hateful motherfucker who wants to burn our house down. Which forced us to relocate. We bring in millions of dollars a year selling weed. And, we're about to lose it all because of this bullshit. My absence should not be taken lightly. I have eyes and ears everywhere now. We have a mole in here and you will be discovered and dealt with harshly. Loyalty is everything in my crew. Disrespect will only be met by death. For real, lies and dishonesty won't be tolerated. I've continued to run Corporate G Enterprise because we are family. Family sticks together. The Marijuana industry is a three billion dollar industry and we have a piece of it. The decisions we make today will determine if we stay in it or if we all get locked up. My mom is sick, so I have to stay longer. Everyone knows their position. Either play it or get the fuck off the field. When I find out who the motherfucker is trying to bring my family down, I will not hesitate to smoke their ass."

The room went silent. Then the phone hung up. Everyone at the table was quite. They only stared at each other.

Minutes later, they started leaving one by one. Nisha tried to phone Ramon back, but never got an answer. She wasn't upset. She understood where he was coming from and she loved him. She and Cory talked about loyalty a lot growing up. And, it seemed to her Cory passed it on to Ramon.

Vonshee, Nisha, and J-Dub were the only ones left. Nisha eyed J-Dub then finally asked. "Have you seen Bree, J-Dub?"

"Honestly, I haven't seen her after she dumped me." J-Dub said.

"Where do you live, Jay?" Vonshee asked, with arms folded.

"What the fuck? What kind of question is that? Y'all plan on cheating on y'all boyfriends or something?" J-Dub laughed.

"Boy, stop. We just asking?" Nisha said. "I received a text after an event you can say. It's like I'm being watched or something."

J-Dub ginned. "I don't think that girl is stalking you."

"Why would you say that?" Nisha asked.

"Dated her and I think she'll stalk me before she stalks you."

"Yeah, but jealousy will make you do some crazy shit," Nisha said, eyeing Rasheem strolling into the office.

"Naw, love, jealousy, envy and money will make you do some crazy shit," J-Dub said, "Trust me. And, I do agree with one of Ramon's sayings. Family is supposed to suppose stick together." J-Dub held up his hand to Rasheem, signaling him to wait.

"Yeah, you're right," Nisha said.

"I'm always right, Nisha. Like that night you slapped me," J-Dub said as he typed away at his phone.

"Who you texting?" Vonshee asked.

"Damn, are these 21 Questions, Where's 50 Cent?" J-Dub looked up and smiled at Vonshee. "If you must know that was Charles. He told me to be ready for a big drop. He want me to ride with him."

"Vonshee, he's lying?" Nisha said.

"I'm not. Call him and ask. But, I have to go right now. I see y'all tomorrow. I gotta get some shit done today," J-Dub said, walking out with Rasheem.

*****

The following morning, Fantasia received a call from Ramon. She was just finishing up her nics and nacs to a program she'd put together.

"What's up, Fanny?"

"Hey Ramon. So, I got the Corporate G Enterprise screen up. Plus, I have all the shell companies who washes our money."

"Okay, that's good."

"On one screen I have a list of all the shell companies. I made one more CGE company with a Costa Rica bank account. After I press enter, the funds will be evenly distributed to all ten companies and sent to their accounts. You have $20 million, that's two million in each account."

"Ten shells? I can work with that," Ramon said.

Fantasia laughed. "Well, anyway. Every two hours for the next forty eight hours the money will bounce around in a web, intersecting each other until they all reach the center. The companies are located in Marocco, Mexico, Cuba, The Virgin Islands, and Switzerland. That's two companies for each country. After the forty eight hours the fund will shoot to one account, the Costa Rica account. The only people who can access these funds are the names you gave me, last night."

"You truly are a beast, Fanny?"

"I know, sometimes I surprise myself."

"I love you, Fanny."

Fantasia laughed. "You better. We need an exit plan now."

"Like what?" Ramon replied.

"I don't know. Remember you're the brain. I'm just the tech."

"I'll come up with something. Now press that enter key."

"Anything you say, Boss," Fantasia said, pressing the enter key on her MacBook.

CHAPTER 15 – S.W.A.T

Charles headed to the bank to drop off a deposit of $125,000 into one of the operation's bank accounts. It was something Ramon trained them to always do to make the business legit. Charles reached the local bank, fetched his Gucci bag from the backseat and went inside.

Minutes later, Charles exited the back after taking care of all his bank business. He pulled out of the parking lot and stopped at a traffic light.

Looking in the rearview mirror, he saw what looked like to be a rental making all the stops and turns he did.

"I know this bullshit car is not following me," he said.

He continued driving the speed limit until he reached 610 and Stella Link. He yielded slowly and jumped on the interstate, then he mashed on the gas. His Lexus Sport shot into traffic. The following vehicle was no match for the made for speed sports car.

*****

Detective Knowles took her seat as her partner called her task force into the meeting room. She also welcomed Detective Black. She had developed a plan to force Ramon and his crew out of hiding. Knowles never told her partner about the meeting she had between her and Ramon's tech. She knew the crew was highly advanced and felt any plan would never work. She had lots of doubts.

"Okay, everybody." Lopez began, "The Mayor made this a priority case. We discovered the grow house in

THE PRETTY DIVA STORY

the South Meadows neighborhood belongs to Cory Beaudruex. He was shot almost two years ago. His operation kept going after his murder. Why?" she asked, glancing around the room.

"Because his right hand man, Ramon Dumas took it over. We believe Dumas knows something about Cory's death. He is now our prime suspect. The murder case went cold until the fire. But, now we have three cases linked together and the Houston Police Department must take action to solve them," Lopez finished like a motivational speaker.

Black laughed.

Shocked, Lopez asked, "Is there something funny, Black?"

"Is that all you have?" he chuckled.

"At the time, yes."

"Well, if I may speak, Detective. I've been doing my own investigation on this also. Dumas had a second grow house and he moved it recently before we almost found its location," Black said.

Knowles yelled from the back. "How'd you find it?"

"One of my Confidential Informants. He also told me Dumas's current girlfriend has been making sure things run smoothly while he's gone."

"Any info on his girlfriend?" Knowles asked.

"Yes, that's the good part," Detective Black said. "Her name is Ronisha Beaudruex.

Everyone in the room gasped.

Knowles was even more shocked, knowing she knew Cory's last name sounded familiar. When she heard Ronisha's name come out of Black's mouth, her mind went to spinning. "That can't be Ronisha from high school," she said under her breath.

Black turned to the meeting. "I also arrested Charles Lyons. Busted him for moving cocaine. And guess who bonded him out?"

"Who?"' Lopez asked.

"Vonshee Jolivette and Ramon Dumas," Black said with a grin.

Knowles stared at Black in even more shock, recognizing the name Vonshee shocked her as well. "What the fuck?"' she asked herself in a low pitch.

Lopez's eyes pierced at Black as if they could speak. Probably wondering, why what was he doing at a traffic stop? "Well, we need to locate Mr. Lyons," Lopez said closing her folder.

"I agree," Black said. "But we don't have his address or any location on him."

"No, we don't. But we have a court date," Lopez said, stepping down from the podium.

"He'll be with his lawyer. You think he'll speak with us?" Knowles asked.

"Maybe not, but it's worth a try," Lopez said, exiting the room.

*****

Rasheem and J-Dub were packing up when Rasheem looked at J-Dub. "Can I ask you a question, Jay?"

"You already did, but you can ask me another one."

"Have you ever read the 48 Laws of Power and the 33 Strategies of War?"

"I haven't fully read through both of them. But I have read enough."

"That's cool. One of my favorite laws, I can't really recall. But the book said to use smoke screens to conceal your intentions. By the time your enemy figures out what happened, you've basically accomplished what you needed when the smoke clears."

"Are you the smoke screen?" J-Dub asked,

Rasheem laughed. "Naw, but we both could be one. Anyone can be one."

"What other laws have you read?" J-Dub asked.

"Well, another law of Robert Green is to destroy your enemies completely, My top one is to never outshine the master."

J-Dub studied Rasheem for a moment. "I did read those chapters. But who is your master?"

"Well, if I really had to pick. I would say it's money for right now."

J-Dub nodded his head. "You no what lil bro, I like that answer. So help me with these bags and then let's get you paid."

Rasheem smiled, rubbing his hands together. "Now, you're speaking my language, big bro."

*****

Detective Knowles was back at her desk when she received a call from Chief Taylor. "Where the hell are you in this case? I've just received word the FBI are about to get involved for some reason. They're giving us a week to get our shit together. This grow house case has gained too much media attention."

"We found out Dumas hasn't been in the state in the last month. His operation is currently being ran by his girlfriend."

"What a surprise?" the Chief said with sarcasm.

"I know, Chief, but what we found out was shocking. His new girlfriend is Cory's little sister, Ronisha Beaudruex."

"Wait, what? Are you serious?"

"Yes?"

"Wow, these cases just keep getting better. Keep digging, I want this over with. Let's solve this before the FBI take this from us," the Chief demanded.

CHAPTER 16 – THE TRIANGLE

For the first time in weeks, Fantasia was at her double screen workplace. Her sanctuary. She was working on the hard drive she and Nisha found at the grow house. The titanium box was burned around the edges and the ports were melted. She sent the hard drive to her hardware tech, Steven, who took it apart and rebuilt it. The memory card was undamaged like she had hoped. After plugging in the drive, Fantasia watched it load up to the computer.

She was skilled enough to pull up deleted files and retrieve lost data. She found a password protected file she didn't create and connected a password decoder.

In minutes, the decoder broke the code. Before opening it, she sent the file to the Sand Box in case it had a virus.

She opened it and no virus was in it. "Yes," Fantasia said.

Fantasia browsed through the hard drive until reaching the security files for all of the installed cameras inside the grow house. She opened them and realized the cameras saved every three hours. She scrolled through the video files until she reached one with the grow house fire date on it. She clicked the link and eventually three masked intruders with hoodies appeared. They stole from the grow house and the whole robbery took thirty minutes. Before leaving, they poured gasoline everywhere and lit it.

*****

Nisha touched down in LAX and called herself an Uber to take her to the Marriott, where she had booked a room for the weekend. Nisha never told Ramon she was coming to town. She had surprises for him. Something they both could enjoy. After settling down, all she wanted to do was shop. Her first stop, Victoria's Secret

*****

Ramon was planning his exit. Law enforcements were getting close. He sensed it. '20 million dollars. I really could call it quits right now. But, I'm feeding so many people,' he thought.

His phone rang. It was Nisha

"What are you doing, Babe?" Nisha asked.

"I just left my mom's house. I had to drive her home after her chemo session."

"Awww, that's so sweet of you. I want to see you. Then, maybe later you can take me to meet her. Because I'm in Cali."

"Stop playing."

"For real, flew in earlier," Nisha began, "You know I like to eat. So, picked me up tonight. I have two surprises for you."

"Well, if you're serious. I know a spot. I'll pick you up around eight."

"I'm at the Downtown Marriott."

"Cool, I'll call you back when I'm on my way. I have to swing by the dispensary."

"Alright, Love," Nisha said.

THE PRETTY DIVA STORY

"We'll be waiting."

Before Ramon could respond, Nisha hung up. He didn't mind. He had other business to attend to. He called Charles and asked, "What you got going on?"

"Doing a quick drop," Charles answered.

"Yo, Nisha made a surprise trip out here. Is Vonshee with her?"

"Naw, Vonshee's with me."

"Really? Because she said we'll be waiting?"

"She probably was just talking fast," Charles said, laughing. "When are you coming back to the city?"

"I really can't say. Fantasia suggested that I stay away for a little bit longer. You know how she is about me."

"Yeah, I know. Plus we're hot like Hot Boy's album," Charles joked. "Man, I think I was being followed the other day. I lost them in traffic."

"Did you get a look at the driver?" Ramon asked.

"Not really, but the next motherfucker who follow me will end up in an ICU."

Ramon laughed. "Yeah, I know. Look at what happened to the last dude you popped. I'll. call you tomorrow to check up on things."

*****

Later that night, Nisha and Ramon were done with their meals at Gabby's, a high end restaurant right outside of Hollywood. The restaurant received national attention after singer songwriter Rosa Rodanne shot a video there. It went viral overnight.

"Here's one of your surprises," Nisha said, pushing a box in front of him.

Ramon opened it and pulled out a Cuban link chain with a name plate with VVS Diamonds in it. Ramon admired the piece as it twinkled in the light. He leaned over giving Nisha a long passionate kiss. "Thanks boo, but you really didn't have to."

They finished their dinner and left back to the Marriott.

Ramon stopped Nisha before walking into the room. "Before we go in, I need to know two things. One, you said we'll be waiting earlier on the phone. And, number two, you said you have two surprises for me. Where's the second one?" he asked, smiling.

Nisha giggled. "Well, I didn't get to enjoy my birthday the way I wanted to. So, I've decided to bring the party to you."

"Why would I need a party? It was your birthday."

"I didn't get to enjoy it the way I wanted to," Nisha said, slipping the key into the slot. She opened the door to be beautiful Latina laying in the king size bed.

Ramon looked at Nisha with confusion on his face. "What the hell?"

"Yup, let's go," Nisha said, pushing him inside.

Ramon asked no questions as the sexy Latina approached them.

"Ramon, this is my friend, Selena," Nisha said, kissing him on the cheek.

Ramon rocked up instantly.

"*Vamanos, Papi*," Selena said, pulling him by the hand and escorting him to the bed.

Selena was dressed in a see through two piece lingerie that Nisha picked out earlier. Selena pushed Ramon onto the bed and both women settled down in between his legs. Selena unzipped his pants while Nisha pulled out his manhood *"Esta Grande!"* Selena said, rubbing him up and down his 8 inch shaft.

Both women took turns pulling on him. Nisha held him with a firm grip while her friend bobbed her head on his tip. Ramon was mesmerized as he watched in pleasure. The wet slurping noises from Selena's mouth filled the room. The saliva lubricate dripping from her lips made the oral sex even more blissful. Selena pushed him as far as she could, and gagged as tears ran down her face. Nisha wiped them away like a true caring friend. After watching Selena show off her throat skills, Nisha prepared herself to do the same. Nisha wrapped her mouth around Ramon's girth and worked her way up and down his manhood. When she was done pleasing her man, she ordered Selena to position herself between her legs. Selena listened like a trained sex slave. After receiving her pleasure from Selena, they put a XL magnum condom on Ramon as he watched wide eyed.

"First, you do her and then you do me," Nisha said as Selena turned around and put her hips in the air.

"Damn," Ramon said as he positioned himself behind what looked to be forty inches of pure Latina thickness. He pushed himself inside her slowly as she moaned. Nisha settled under Selena's tongue . The licks from her tongue made Nisha's head snapped back. Ramon penetrated Selena and watched Nisha, who was seeming to be in another world. Ramon pumped harder and faster. He gripped her waist and pounded her with intense strokes. She moaned sexually and intensely. After reaching multiple orgasms she pulled away from him and collapsed on top of the bed.

"Aww, *Mamacita*, it's my turn. I want some too," Nisha said, positioning herself to receive her hard pounding.

"You ready?" Ramon asked, putting himself behind his girlfriend.

"Yes, Daddy, I want it all," she said, reaching and removing his magnum condom allowing him slide in and feeling his legs get weak. "Damn, this is good."

Nisha looked back and smiled as she rocked back and forward intensively until she climaxed. After Nisha's pleasure from behind, Ramon picked her up and made love to her in the air as Selena watched, pleasing herself. When he was done giving Nisha the pounding she deserved, he sat down on the bed still hard inside of her. Nisha pushed out moans as she felt all 8 inches pulsating inside of her. She began to bounce and grind as Selena made her way to Ramon's face. Selena and Nisha kissed passionately while Selena rode his tongue like a wild horse. Both women grind on him, twerking and working him until they all three reached their sexual peaks. They rose off of him in sync. Ramon was dripping in sweat as he stood up. He ordered both women to sit next to each other in doggy-style position. He stared at both women in front of him, amazed at the view.

"Hell yeah," he said as he watched Nisha spread Selena's cheeks. He grabbed her by the hips and pushed his shaft inside of her again.

Selena moaned, "*Aye, Papi,* Fuck me." Her latin words only encouraged him to buck harder. He felt her shake and took that as a sign of doing his job.

Afterwards, he pushed her forward and stepped to the side where Nisha was waiting with her hips still in the air. He loved seeing his girl on all fours. Ramon slid in slowly as Nisha gasped in ecstasy. He stroked her as she turned to Selena for a kiss to help stop her from screaming. His girth was a perfect match for her tightness. Nisha rocked back and forward trying to keep up with his tempo. Ramon smacked her ass and rammed her hard. "Fuck me, Daddy," Nisha moaned.

Ramon smiled and stroked faster as she cried out. He fed her well. And, the sounds of cheeks lapping against him helped build up an intense climax. He could feel it approaching. It was knocking hard and both women were there to answer. "Oh, shit I'm about to come," he said, tightening his teeth. Nisha arched her back and slowly pulled away. She turned around with Selena there and they staked him together until he couldn't take the pleasure no more "I want you to unload all over me, Papi," Selena said, licking her lips

"You sure, *Mami?*" Nisha asked, stroking Ramon more intensely.

Selena smiled. "*Por Favor.*"

"Here it comes," Ramon said as Selena positioned herself to receive her prize.

"Oh shit," he moaned out.

Nisha stroked him as he released himself all over Selena's beautiful Latina face. Selena was determined to get every drop and with Nisha's help, she accomplished just that.

After climaxing, Ramon was exhausted. He hit the bed, panting. Both women, satisfied, collapsed right next to him. All three amazed and drained, past out holding each other.

CHAPTER 17 – MEMBERSHIP

The next morning, Ramon stood outside on Nisha's hotel room balcony. Still dazed from the night before. He wondered if the sex really happened. He was worth millions, his girlfriend was a ride or die chick, his crew was that eating good and the only thing' through his life off, was the fact detectives were trying to question him about his friend's murder. Nisha came up from behind and put her arms around him. They both stared into the city of Los Angeles. "This is a beautiful view," Nisha said.

"Sure is," he agreed with a smile.

"Did you enjoy last night?" Nisha asked, squeezing him.

"Hell yeah, where did you find Selena?"

Nisha laughed. "Let's just say her Puerto Rican or Cuban ass found me. We met before you and I got serious. She's a down ass chick. I think she's in love with me too."

"Ain't that some shit?"

"Can we keep her?" Nisha asked like a child who just found a lost puppy.

"Do you really need my approval?"

"Yes, Daddy."

Ramon laughed. "Well, yes, you can keep her." He was in love with her. How could he tell her no, especially when it benefited him also.

"Are you two talking about me like I'm a lost baby pit-bull or something?" Selena asked from behind in a Spanish accent.

Ramon and Nisha turned and laughed. "No," Nisha said. "I would never do that to your sexy ass."

"Well, anyways, Mr. Ramon, Nisha has told me so much about you. I feel like I already knew you."

"Is that right," Ramon asked, smiling at Nisha.

"*Si, Papi.* And I think everything she's said is correct. I've been dying to meet you. I met Nisha at one of my jobs and I fell in love at first sight. Okay, that was a lie, *lo siento.* But, I do think she's a beautiful woman. She reminds me of that one singer."

"Yes, I agree," he said, staring at Nisha's Beyonce look-alike features.

"Anyways," Nisha said, cutting in. "I wanted the meeting to be perfect."

"It doesn't get any more perfect than that," Ramon said, grinning.

"So, now what, *Mami*?" Selena asked.

"Yeah, now what?" Ramon asked as Nisha walked over to Selena and hugged her tightly.

"Well, you can be our spicy Latina lover. We don't do anything unless we all agree to it. So, the decision is yours, Ramon. What do you say? You want a triangle relationship?"

Ramon stared Nisha down in shock. "Are y'all serious?"

Nisha and Selena smiled. "Serious like a heart attack," Selena said.

Ramon laughed. "I think this is all a setup. I'm not answering nothing like that. I don't want to give the wrong answer."

"I'll answer for him," Nisha said and paused for a moment. "Yes."

"What the fuck just happened?" Ramon asked.

Nisha giggled. "Your girl got a girlfriend. And, she's officially a Diva. I can't wait to introduce you to the rest of the Pretty Divas."

"Pretty Divas?" Selena asked.

"Yup, I'll fill you in on it the way back to Houston."

*****

Knowles was getting her hair done when she noticed someone walking by with a grey hoodie. She excused herself and went after who she thought could be a suspect.

"What do you want?" a homeless woman said after she turned around.

"I'm sorry I thought you were someone I knew."

"I need ten dollars for bothering me."

"Huh, okay," Knowles answered, reaching into her pocket and giving the lady a ten dollar bill.

"Next time, It'll cost you twenty," she said, showing a toothless smile.

"I'm so sorry," Knowles said as she turned around to walk back to the salon. When Knowles's appointment was over, she walked outside and called Lopez.

"Hello." Lopez answered.

"I missed your call earlier. I was getting my hair done. Anything new?"

"Not yet."

"Where are you?" Knowles asked. "It sounds really quiet."

"Let's just say, I'm close by."

"Well, I'm sorry but I have something to tell you," Knowles sighed.

"What is it?" Lopez asked.

"I had a meeting with the tech from Ramon's crew. She hacked my computer and said if I wanted to talk to her alone. So I did, she disabled my phone, and she knew everything about me,"

Lopez paused. "First off, that's a rookie's mistake. You should never do that again. I'm your partner. If someone wants to meet up, you should always let me know. You never know what type of person you're dealing with. It could have been a set up."

"Yeah, I know, partner," Knowles replied.

"Did she provide anything?"

"Not really, but I do know she's the reason why they stay ten steps ahead of us. She helps cover all of their tracks."

"Well, if she's that good. We need to fight fire with fire. The first move in chess always start with a pawn," Lopez said.

"Well, usually that is true. But who is the first pawn?"

"Come on, rookie," Lopez said, "You should know this"

Knowles smiled. "Rasheem Rahati."

CHAPTER 18 – KNOWLES

"It was reckless. I couldn't help myself," Black said into his cellphone. "I'm a Detective. I'm the one who's been keeping the heat away. So, I'll suggest keeping you watch your tone boy."

"Just calm down," the familiar voice said. "I understand, somethings are hard to resist."

"What do you have for me?" Black asked, calming down some.

"So far, Ramon is still out town and there's been no sign of his girlfriend."

"And, what the hell am I suppose to do with that?" Black asked angrily.

"I've infiltrated the organization like you told me to. The agreement is to report intel to you for payment."

Detective Black hissed. "Just give me something worth the money. I need a location of their new place of business."

"Oh, I have that information and if you weren't so quick to snap at me I would have told you that."

"He'll, give it to me. I'll get a D.A. to have a Judge sign a warrant."

"What? Why? You usually just go all in."

"I have too many infractions on me right now. Sometimes you have to play by the rules." Black said.

The familiar voice released the information. "I have to head back. But tell the new wife I said hello."

"Ha, nice try, boy," Black laughed as he hung up his phone. After Black hung up, he called a D.A. who was just as crooked as he was.

"Well, well, well. You have to be calling for favor," the D.A. answered.

"Yes, Tony. But this one will help us both," Black replied.

"This better be good, Black."

"The grow house fire case that's been catching national attention for the past six months. The one social media has been making a mockery of ever since it made headlines. I've just received intel on the operations and I have it's location."

"You have?"

"Would I lie to you?" Black asked.

The D.A. laughed uncontrollably. "I'll see if I can get you a warrant for a raid."

"Good, I promise you won't be disappointed."

*****

Detective Lopez was at her desk when she received a call from an unknown caller. "Hello, can I help you?"

"If I have info about a crime or a case that was already committed, could I still be compensated?" the caller asked.

"It depends," Lopez said.

The unknown caller was silent for a moment, then spoke. "Well, I have a homegirl who invited me to this guys house. We were all hanging out this past weekend. This guy got totally wasted. He stared yelling and bragging how he and his brother brunt that grow house down. He even said he and his brother started their own operation from the equipment they stole. He said his brother was a mastermind and no one would ever guess who was behind everything."

Lopez sat up straight in her chair. "If you don't mind me asking. Do you have the name of this person?"

"Yeah, if I could remember correctly. My friend said his name was Rasheem. I think I'm pronouncing it right."

"And, where were you and your friend?"

"We went to Rasheem's house. My friend, Diamond, dates his brother. She was trying to hook me up with him. But something didn't seem right about him."

"Do you remember the address?" Lopez asked, grabbing a pen and paper.

"Sure, it was 1770 South Airport Lane."

"Okay, thanks ma'am. We will contact you if this case gets solved or if it leads to a conviction. Can I get your contact information?"

"Huh, you know what? On the secondhand. I'm okay," the caller said as she hung up.

Lopez called Knowles and explained what happened. She told Knowles she would pick her up on the way to Rasheem's house.

A hour later, both detectives knocked on the front door. After not getting an answer, Knowles noticed a shadow in the window. The shadow disappeared. The detectives drew their weapons. Knowles was told to cover while Lopez made her way to the back of the house. Lopez reached the corner of the brick home and a shadow shot passed her out the back door. A small male figure headed toward the gate. Lopez chased him down. As the male tried to jump over the gate, Lopez grabbed his legs, holding on with all her might. Knowles finally made it and grabbed his other leg as both women pulled him off of the gate.

After hitting the ground, Knowles slapped the handcuffs on him and yelled in his face, "You fucking kicked me, bastard."

"I didn't mean to," the young man shouted back.

"Shut up and get your ass up," Lopez said. She searched him and pulled out his wallet from his back pocket. She threw it to Knowles.

Knowles opened it. "Well, look at that. Mr. Rasheem Rahati. We have some questions for you so you know you're coming with us."

They drove through the heavy traffic of Houston until they made it to the Hall.

Rasheem sat still in the interrogation room for a whole hour before Lopez walked in and slammed the door behind her. She threw a thick manilla envelope on the table.

"What's that?" Rasheem asked.

"You're going down, buddy. I hope you know that already."

"For what?" Rasheem asked with a twisted face.

"Arson."

"I don't know anything about arson," Rasheem said, leaning back in his chair and crossing his arms.

"Well, we heard you had a little too much to drink and started talking a little too much. You burned down that grow house. Maybe, because of envy, greed or just plain jealousy," Lopez said.

Rasheem laughed. "Everybody lies about things they didn't do."

"That's true, but you knew Cory and Ramon. And I think you know what happened to that grow house."

"I guess," Rasheem smirked.

"You know all this is a connection, Rasheem."

Detective Knowles walked in.

"Lopez, I have something for you."

Lopez stood up and received a package, then sat back down and opened it. She thumbed through the photos and placed them in front of Rasheem.

Rasheem eyed the photos and smiled. "You're showing me these, because?"

"I just want you to see your aftermath," Lopez said.

"Stop it. I told you before, I don't know anything about that."

"We also know you run for Ramon," Knowles said.

Rasheem slowly turned his head. "I work for myself. I do what I choose."

Reaching inside of the manilla envelope again, Lopez pulled out a Glock 17.

"I see you like playing with little pistols. This was taken from your home. We know it's not registered to you. So, tell us where you got it from."

"I don't remember," Rasheem said. "How you get in my house?"

"You know if we do a ballistic on this gun and find out it's linked to a body. You will be charged." Knowles said, pointing at the gun.

Rasheem paused. "Okay, I bought it off the streets. You bitches should already know that."

"Okay, since you're talking. Where is Ramon?" Lopez asked.

"How should I know?"

"You can play hard-ball if you want or you can make this a lot easier. You help us and we'll make this arson charge go away," Lopez said, smiling.

Tilting his head, Rasheem said, "You're bluffing."

Lopez closed the envelope. "The house is gone, you hit an officer, and all we want from you, is Ramon's location."

Rasheem sat in silence for a little while. "So, you're telling me, if I let you know where Ramon is, you'll let me walk. You basically want me to snitch."

"Let's just say, you're helping us help you," Lopez said.

"Okay, Ramon is in California visiting his sick mother. Supposedly, he's returning in a week."

"Did he fly?" Lopez asked.

"I don't know," Rasheem replied. "I guess so."

Lopez stood up. "Let's go, Knowles."

"So I can go also?" Rasheem asked.

Lopez laughed. "No, why would you think such a thing?"

"Because you said if I told you where Ramon was, I could walk."

"Yes, meaning you can walk on the arson charge. You're free on that but, you still resisted arrest and assaulted an officer. Those, my friend, are charges I can't help you with."

"Unless you turn state and work for me," Lopez said.

"What? You want me to be your snitch?"

"When you say it like that, you make it sound so harsh. I prefer the term Confidential Informant. It rolls off the tongue better."

"I don't know about that," Rasheem said, dropping his head into his hand.

"Well look, my partner and I are going to pay some bills and let you think about it. We'll come and check up on you in a little bit," Lopez said as she walked toward the door.

*****

Fantasia arrived at the warehouse as usual to do her security check. She gathered all the hard-drive's memory from the security system and headed out. On her way to the exit door, she was met by Charles.

"Hey, Fantasia," Charles said.

"Hey Buddy," Fantasia replied. "What have you been up to?"

"I've been busy."

"That's good news, " Fantasia said, smiling.

"Can I ask you a question?"

"Shoot."

"Have you ever loved someone, but you couldn't tell them?"

"Yeah, I can say I have but, why are you asking me a question like that?"

"Honestly, going through some things."

"Charles, if you really love someone, then you should tell them the best you know how. You should be there for them the best way you can no matter if you're with that person of not."

Charles shook his head. "I mean, I guess you're right."

Fantasia smiled and gave him a hug. "Since I have you right here. I want to show you something. I was going to wait until Ramon got back but, I'll show you first."

Fantasia turned on her tablet and pulled up the grow house fire footage.

Charles leaned over and watched the video then asked Fantasia to rewind it. He studied the robbers. "Wait a minute. I know that walk," he said. "And, I think you do have too."

Fantasia looked up. "Yes, my first thought was, Rasheem."

"That's who I thought. That son of a bitch."

"We have to call Ramon."

"No, just be cool. I'll handle everything and I'll tell Ramon."

"What do you have planned, Charles?" Fantasia asked, turning off her tablet.

"We're going to play along. I'ma play his rat game, then I'ma call in an exterminator."

Fantasia chuckled. "Boy, you're crazy. Just be careful. Don't need you catching no more bodies."

"Oh, I will be careful."

"Well, I'm headed home to look at these other files. I'll call you later to check up on you," Fantasia said as she walked out of the door. She could also sense something was wrong with Charles. She wondered if she should have shown him the security footage especially knowing who dangerous he could be when ever he gets mad. Charles had already killed somebody and beat the murder charge.

*****

Nisha and Selena were getting ready to fly back to Houston. Ramon sat on the hotel's sofa watching as Nisha and Selena joked and played with each other. He thought to himself. 'Now, I understand why Future said Life's Good.'

Minutes later, Ramon dropped off both women at LAX. When Nisha exited the car, her phone beeped. It was a text from another random number. She passed the phone to Ramon and he read the text. 'First the peasants, next the Queen, then the King.'

"What the fuck is this?" he asked.

"I have no idea, Babe," Nisha answered.

Ramon shook his head. "It's cool. I'll be home in two weeks. We'll get to the bottom of all this bullshit."

Nisha grabbed her phone. "I'm not even going to respond to this."

"Good, " Ramon said. "Do me a favor. Call me when you touch down."

Before departing from each other, Ramon gave Nisha a kiss goodbye and hugged Selena. Then, he watched both women walk through the airport's door holding each hands and swinging their hips.

*****

Meanwhile back in Houston, Detective Knowles sat at her desk, thinking, "Is the world is really this small?" She and Nisha had done so much together in high school. She was after Ramon and his crew and now, it seems she's after her childhood friend also. It seemed Nisha has done well for herself, even though she was supplying the streets with weed. Knowles had to admit, she was a little proud of her childhood friend. She also wondered about Fantasia. Where did they get that woman from? Right at that moment, Knowles's phone rang. She looked down at it and saw a familiar number.

"Hello, Knowles speaking. How can I help you?"

"How are you, Detective?" Fantasia asked.

"I'm fine, what about you?"

"I'm doing well. I have something for you and it's coming through to you via Gmail. I'll wait while you check it."

Knowles check her email and was shocked after pressing play and watching the video with the mask intruders burn down Ramon's grow house.

"We already know who burned down the grow house," Knowles said.

"I'm pretty sure you do. I'm sure you're looking for the other two intruders also. If my friend was trying to take over Cory's operation. Why would he burn it down?" Fantasia asked.

"I understand you want to help Ramon, but the only way he can truly clear his name is if he speaks to us. Getting involved will only hurt him."

Fantasia went silence momentarily. "Tell Mr. Rahati to stay away from us. He is no longer welcomed."

Before Knowles could reply, Fantasia hung up.

"What happened?" Lopez asked, walking over to Knowles.

"That was Ramon's tech, Lori Johnson aka Fantasia."

"What did she say?"

"We'll she sent me a link to a video of three robbers robbing and burning the grow house down six months ago. And she requested I tell Mr. Rahati to stay away from their crew."

"She threatened him?"

"It sounded more like a warning."

"How did she know we picked him up?" Lopez asked.

"Assuming that she's a highly trained hacker. I can't really say."

"Knowles, call Mr. Rahati and tell him to lay low until we tell him different. And warn him not to do anything stupid, just act normal."

Knowles nodded in agreement.

"I'll call Black and see where he's at on this also." Lopez added.

*****

Detective Black was in another world when he received a call from Detective Lopez. He quickly wiped his nose off, it was residue from the most purest cocaine in the city.

"What is it?" Black answered.

"Black we have a problem. Ramon's crew figured out we have intel on them and they found out we have an inside on them." Knowles said.

Black laughed and said nothing.

"Are you okay, Black?" Knowles asked.

"Yeah, I was just thinking. Maybe we need to move in on them before they get too slick."

"You mean an unauthorized raid without a warrant?"

"I already have a warrant signed," Black said in a low voice.

"Okay, I'll inform Lopez."

"Yeah, you do that."

Knowles sighed. "Are you sure you're okay, Black?"

"I told you, I was okay. Just tell her to call me so I can give her all the info so she can set up everything and get her task force together."

"Okay, calm down," Knowles said before she hung up.

*****

Hours later, Nisha and Selena arrived in Houston. Bush Continental Airport was packed and busy as usual. The women parted ways minutes before Vonshee pulled up to pick up Nisha.

"You had fun?" Vonshee asked, smiling.

"Yeah, couldn't have asked for a better vacation," Nisha replied.

"I'm headed to Fantasia's house. You want to roll?"

"Sure," Nisha said, rolling her window down.

Half an hour later, Vonshee pulled into Fantasia's apartment complex parking lot.

"Did y'all miss me?" Nisha asked, smiling and settling down on Fantasia's sofa.

Fantasia and Vonshee turned to each other. "Girl Stop," Vonshee said.

"Well, I missed y'all too."

Fantasia stood up and walked to her computer screen. "Since I have both of you ladies here. I want to show you two things. I've been working on this all night."

"Really?" Vonshee asked.

"Yup," Fantasia said, pointing to her laptop screen. "This is the case database for the HPD homicide department. They stop working on your brother's case six months after he was shot. The case went cold. It was recently dug out of the cold case files when the Narcotics and Vice Department discovered the grow house was linked to Cory's name."

"Okay, but why are you telling me this. I already know this," Nisha said.

"I mean No Man's Land is off limits. No one ever goes there unless it's for bad intentions. There's nothing but land out there."

"Which means?" Vonshee asked.

"Well, first let me tell you this. The officer who supposedly found your brother's body was Detective Jeremy Black. He was first at the scene. The only problem is, how did he even know a body was in the area?"

Nisha read through the files while Fantasia talked. "It says here, it was two different tire marks at the scene," Nisha said, pointing at the screen.

"Which means there was foul play," Fantasia said.

"Yeah. Someone else was there," Nisha added.

"You're exactly right boo. I think there covering up something."

CHAPTER 19 - DISMISSED

Charles sat in the office of Mr. Chaney nervous. His attorney, a smart man with ties to the streets walked in with a straight face. He wore a suit from the Steve Harvey Collection.

"Well, Mr. Lyons, I have good news and I have bad news. Which one of the two do you want to hear first?" Mr. Chaney asked.

Charles turned to Vonshee, who sat in silence with her arms folded. "We will take the bad news first."

"Okay, Mr. Lyons, something went wrong with your case. I've filed motions that forced the courts to turn over evidence to me. We've discovered the kilo of cocaine you were arrested for never made it to the evidence room. When I asked about it, I was met with silence."

Vonshee's face lit up. "Okay, so what does that mean?"

"My only conclusion was that one of the two men who arrested Mr. Lyons never logged it into the evidence room. Which means someone is a dirty cop."

"And what's the good news? Because that don't sound to bad."

"The good news is one of them will have to answered for a kilo of missing coke," the lawyer answered.

"Really!?" Charles asked.

"Yes, and Mr. Lyons, you never told me that they never read you your rights. I viewed the squad car cam and found that out myself. They illegally searched you and your vehicle so the D.A. has agreed to drop the charges."

"Are you serious?" Charles asked with a smirk.

"So, you're saying he's free?" Vonshee added.

"As of right now, Mr. Lyons is a free man."

"What about the two officers who arrested me?" Charles asked as his lawyer took off his glasses and sat them on his desk.

"Mr. Lyons, my strong recommendation would be to move on from this. You got extremely lucky. Let dirty law enforcements deal with dirty law enforcements."

"That's advice we can live with," Vonshee said.

Charles and Vonshee both stood up and shook Mr. Chaney's hand.

"It's been a pleasure, Mr. Chaney," Charles said.

"Likewise, it's the least I could do. You did pay me after all."

Once Charles made it to his car, he phoned Ramon to tell him the good news.

"What's up, fam?" Ramon said after he answered.

"Mr. Chaney got the case thrown out."

"I told you he was good," Ramon said.

"When are you returning back to the city?"

"I'll be back pretty soon. My mom's doing a lot better."

"That's good to know."

"Is everything running smoothly out there?"

"You know I got it on lock. And you know Nisha. She's like a little pretty diva pit-bull. She staying on top of her shit."

"Yeah, I know," Ramon chuckled.

"How's the dispensary?" Charles asked, turning the key to his Lexus.

"I can't complain. The state is taxing us, but it's not like we can't afford it. I'm bringing some new seeds with me too. I got some strands that's never been grown before."

"Cool," Charles said. "You need me to do anything for you over here?" Ramon paused.

He thought about his next move, it had to be planned perfectly. "Yeah, I do. I need you to rent me a box truck and do a move for me."

"Why?" Charles asked.

"I'll explain everything to you after you get the truck. And make sure you get the truck in someone else's name."

"I can do that."

"I need this done today."

"Alright. I'll take care of it. I'll call you when everything is handled."

"Good, and tell all the worker's to take off until they receive a call from me."

"That's a bet, let me drop off Vonshee and I'll get right on it."

When Charles was done, he hung up his phone and turned toward Vonshee, who was tapping away at her phone.

"What was that all about?" Vonshee asked, looking down at her iPhone's screen.

Charles shrugged his shoulders. "To be honest, I'm not really sure but he said he'll give me more details later."

CHAPTER 20 - LIFE

Nisha sat on the toilet in the mini mansion's master bedroom bathroom. She had been feeling different ever since she visited Ramon in California.

After feeling tired, throwing up, eating more and even being moody, she suspected she was pregnant. Nisha tapped her hands on her knees as she waited on the pregnancy test to reveal itself. Nisha never really thought about kids ever since her miscarriage with her ex-boyfriend, Brocko.

After a long ten minutes of waiting, it came to no surprise, she and Ramon had created life.

Nisha wanted to call Bree and deliver the news, but Bree was missing in action. A tear fell from her face as she thought about Bree. She wiped it away, attended to her womanly duties, and headed out to do more transactions. The drive around the city helped clear her head. She pulled to the intersection of Westhiemer and Fondren and decided to call Vonshee.

"Vonshee speaking, now it's your turn."

Nisha laughed. "Where are you at?"

Vonshee giggled.

"First, you sound like that old Boost Mobile commercial and second, I'm at the smoke shop."

"Are you super busy?"

"Not really."

Nisha sighed. "Well, I have something to tell you."

"Okay, go ahead."

"Naw, I need to be face-to-face."

"This must be good," Vonshee said.

"You know what, it is. So, I'm just going to tell you. You're going to be a Godmother in about nine months."

"Oh my God! Are you saying you're pregnant, Nisha?" Vonshee asked excitedly?

"Yes," Nisha responded.

"And I'm keeping his little ass."

"His?"

"Yup, you heard me."

Vonshee laughed. "How do you even know it's a boy?"

"Trust me, a mother knows," said with a laugh.

"Girl, stop."

"When do you get off?" Nisha asked.

"Eight o'clock sharp."

"Girl's night at the mansion," Nisha said.

"I can swing by, I was going to go to see Charles, but his ass can wait or take a rain check."

"Good, because I really need my besties right now," Nisha cried.

"Have you told Ramon?"

"Not yet," Nisha said, wiping her eyes.

"Awww, well I'll be there after my shift."

"Okay, call me when you get close," Nisha said before she hung up.

*****

Rasheem laid in his bed staring at the ceiling fan as it spun around and round like a speeding clock. He couldn't believe he got caught by two female cops. He felt he was being used by everyone. Being a C.I. for two different people messed with his head the most. J-Dub had him running around the city on dope runs, he envied Charles and Vonshee's relationship, and now a monkey a wrench had been thrown into his plans. He thought the phone call to Detective Black would've got pretty boy Charles out of the picture. Charles somehow wiggled his way out of a prison sentence. Rasheem slammed his hands on his bed and hissed. He also wanted to hurt the bitch who called him in. He wanted his freedom from everything and everyone's bondage. And cooperating with the police seemed to be his only way out.

Startled by his phone, he looked at his Galaxy and swiped. "Hello,"

A familiar voice came through the ear piece. "Yo, you're burned, we need you to stay away from the operation for a while. You need to lay low."

"What?"

"Look, I've just received word the Feds will be in tomorrow to take over the case. I can't say why at the moment. I'll find out in the morning."

"Should I leave town?" Rasheem asked.

"No, I need you within reach. Just lay low and act normal. A raid is about to happen on the warehouse as we speak. I'll call you soon."

Rasheem's phone was still in his ear. The sound of a raid going down on the warehouse was the sound of magic.

*****

Detective Lopez, Black, Knowles and the rest of the narcotic task force had surrounded Ramon's warehouse. Knowles stood to the left of the entrance. Black went around to the back. He was met by two other members of the team. He signaled the two officers to. bust the door down. The back door busted open and hung off one hinge. Black rushed in followed by the officers. Seconds later, he realized the warehouse had been completely cleared out.

Minutes later, Lopez and Knowles met Black in the back room. Black stood over a folded card.

"Is everything okay, Black?" Knowles asked, holstering her weapon.

"Look at this," Black said as he kneeled.

Lopez and Knowles turn to where Black was glaring. He was focused on the card. Knowles kneeled next to him and picked up the card and read it out loud.

Hello Detectives,
Thank you for playing our treasure hunt.
You have successfully played level one.
Please collect your prize and exit the building.
This is Private Property.
Please watch your step on your way out.
Again, Thanks for playing.

Detective Black gritted his teeth and huffed. He headed toward the door. "Son of a bitch is taunting us," he yelled.

"I must agree with him," Lopez said, running after him.

*****

Detective Knowles directed the officers and ordered them to pack up everything. After getting into her unmarked Crown Vic, she waited for her partner who seemed to be comforting Detective Black. Knowles understood his attitude toward the case and the raid. It was a little embarrassing. Not to mention the explanation he'll have to give to the Chief and the Mayor. This group is really special she thought to herself as Lopez made her way over.

"What do you think about this group?" Knowles asked, smiling as Lopez entered the vehicle.

"They are special. But I have something up my sleeves for them," Lopez said, buckling her seat belt.

Knowles put the car in drive and drove off.

*****

7:30 P.M. glowed on Ramon's digital clock when Nisha returned back to the mansion. The night was getting gloomy and Nisha was exhausted. She wanted to call Ramon and tell him the news, but instead she booked a flight to surprise him once again.

Vonshee knocked on the door at 8:27, Nisha opened it and greeted her long time friend. After giving Nisha a squeeze, Vonshee asked. "Why haven't you told him ?"

"I want to tell him face-to-face," Nisha replied.

"I understand."

"Yeah, I wish Bree was here to get the news also."

"Well, good luck with that," Vonshee said, taking a seat on Ramon's sofa.

Nisha nodded. "She's been missing for almost six months. Do you think she just moved away and doesn't want to mess with us anymore?"

"That's a good theory. But you must have forgot about them bullets flying past your head on your birthday."

"Trust me, I remember," Nisha said as she settled down on the love seat.

"I mean, it looked like a woman," Vonshee said.

"I know, all this shit is just crazy."

Vonshee smiled. "Who are you telling? You're pregnant now, Ramon moved his operation, Charles won't tell me shit that they're working on, and I hate it.

"Where did they move it to?"

"I promised not to say until he's ready to reveal it. I have to respect his request."

Vonshee reached into her purse and pulled out her phone. "Aren't you the loyal one?"

"Yup," Nisha said. "He has assigned people working and attending to the plants so everything is okay."

"J-Dub's been blowing up my phone looking for you. He most likely want to know the location, because Charles ain't saying shit to him either."

Nisha laughed. "Well, he can keep looking. I'm not telling him shit also. My man told me not to tell a soul."

Vonshee grinned. "I wonder what the cops said when they read the note on that card you said you left."

"They probably went nuts. We really need to thank Fantasia's high tech ass. She's the reason we stay on top of everything."

"Yeah, we should," Vonshee said, tapping at her phone.

Nisha leaned over. "Girl, what are you doing?"

Vonshee pulled the phone to her chest. "Nothing."

"Whatever, I'm about to call Fantasia and tell her to come through. Then, I'm going to go cook. I'm hungry."

CHAPTER 21 – GEEK SQUAD 2

Days later, Fantasia drove Nisha to Spybots, the only spy company in the city. Fantasia was fascinated with the store. Once the women were inside.

Fantasia couldn't resist any longer.

"So, you invited me over here a few days ago and didn't tell me the news?"

"What news?" Nisha smiled.

"Girl, don't play. Vonshee already told me. So, is it true?"

"Play?"

"Nisha, are you pregnant?" Fantasia asked, reaching for an USB Card.

"What if I said yes?"

"Then I would most definitely say congratulation."

"Okay, I am, but I'm only three weeks."

"Well, congratulation," Fantasia said. "Have you told Ramon?"

"No, but I will. I already booked a flight back to California."

"Really?"

"Yup, I'll be leaving in the morning so please don't tell him."

"Why would I do such a thing?" Fantasia said, handing Nisha a digital voice recorder.

"What am I supposed to do with this?" Nisha asked, flipping the package around.

"I don't know, boo, you never know though," Fantasia smiled.

After Fantasia and Nisha gathered all the cameras, mini mics, USBs, and computer software, they were helped to the register by a dark skinned woman wearing an employees Spybot shirt.

"Is there anything else I can help you ladies with?" the woman asked.

"Yes, do you guys have long-range walkie-talkies?" Fantasia answered.

"Yes, ma'am, we do. I can show you them."

"Another time," Fantasia said.

Nisha stood at the register and waited, looking around at all the spy gear. She read the back of the voice recorder box. She wanted to know all the specs. Fantasia paid for the products and both women left for Nisha's apartment to mess with all of the equipment. After arriving, Nisha noticed a parked car in the handicap parking space. The car was an unmarked vehicle with Texas exempt license plates. She knew it was a police car. The vehicle slowly backed out and left the apartment complex.

*****

Meanwhile in Downtown Houston, The police force were hosting their newest member to the case. Knowles and Lopez along with the other members of the team eyed the FBI agent as she spoke.

"My name is Special Agent Yazmin Glaze. I can only guess you're wondering why we are here and why we are getting involved in your cases. I can assure you, we're only here to help. I'm here we've discovered that the gun that was used in Cory Beaudruex's murder is a registered police weapon. The shells found in both cases are a match and ballistics records show it's the casing of a Shockwave bullet only given and made for police officers."

Knowles raised her hands and asked," Are you saying a cop killed Cory?"

"No, the registered weapon belongs to Cleveland Lower, a NYPD Officer who was supposedly killed in the line of duty."

"So the weapon was stolen?" Lopez asked.

"Yes, and whoever stole it, either knows Officer Lower or had some kind of connection to him."

Detective Black stood up and walked out of the meeting. "Excuse me, Chief, but I have an important call to make involving my child."

"Are you serious?" the Chief asked. "It can't wait?"

"Honestly, no. It's really important."

"Okay, but hurry."

"Thank you, Chief," Black said, walking off.

*****

Hours had passed, Detective Knowles and Lopez were back at their desks doing more research when Black approached Lopez's desk.

"This isn't a social call," Black said.

Lopez laughed. "I hope not."

"I'm going back to the warehouse. I want to view it up close. Something tells me that we've missed something. Would you like to join me?" he asked.

Lopez turned to him. "Well, since you asked me nicely. I suppose I can join you."

"Okay, let's go," Black said urgently

Lopez grabbed all of her belongings and they headed out the door.

*****

Detective Knowles watched Lopez and Black leave together. She turned to her computer and logged into the police database. She searched the name Cleveland Lower and found out, Mr. Lower was an NYPD Officer who transferred to HPD five years ago and was a partner with Black. She searched and searched, until she found out Chief Taylor had also work" cases with Black before she hid because Chief.

Half an hour later, Knowles watched everyone rush to the television. She followed and pushed her way to the front. She was shocked as she read the headline. 'Massive warehouse fire in Southeast Houston.'

Knowles grabbed her phone and rushed out of the door. The thought of her partner and Black together at the warehouse sent her mind racing. But so did the thought of the crew trying to burn down their last known location.

After pulling out of the Hall's parking lot, she phoned Lopez but only received her voicemail.

CHAPTER 22 - GUESS WHO'S BACK?

Forty-eight hours later Nisha had arrived in California. She wanted to deliver the news to Ramon face-to-face. She was excited as she paid for her room. But she also wondered if Ramon would receive the news in a good way or a bad way. Nevertheless, she prepared everything just like last time she visited minus her spicy Latina friend, Selena.

After preparation, Nisha phoned Ramon, who answered on the third ring.

"What are you doing, Boo?" Nisha asked.

"I'm at the dispensary. What's up?"

"Well, I have something to show and tell you."

"Okay, just Facetime me."

"No, I need to do this in person. Can you meet me at the Downtown Marriott again?"

"What?" Ramon asked, surprised.

"Yup, I'm back in Cali."

Ramon chuckled. "You know I was coming back to Houston in a week. Why you didn't just wait for me?"

"I wanted to see you and you've been saying you're coming back. And have you returned yet?"

Ramon laughed. "Well, you know what's up."

"I do. So, are you coming or not?" Nisha asked.

"Yeah, let me tell my sister and I'll be on my way."

"Alright, that's cool," Ramon said as he hung.

*****

Ramon knocked on Nisha's hotel room door and walked through like the man he knew he was. Not wanting to ruin anything, he avoided all questions. Ramon sat next to his beautiful girlfriend, pulled out an ounce of weed, and asked her to roll it. Nisha pro rolled the marijuana, lite it, and passed it to him. He took several puffs and put his mind as ease.

"Hmmmmm," she said.

"What?"

"It smells like OG Purp."

Ramon smiled, holding the joint. "It's from our newest batch at the shop. You want some?" he asked, putting the weed in her face. She stared at it for a moment then told him, "No, I'm good for now."

A little shocked, he asked, "What's wrong?"

Nisha smiled. "I just don't feel like smoking right now."

"Well, what do you feel like doing?"

Nisha sat up and thought about it for a moment. Then, she reached over and grabbed the joint, put it out and climbed on top of him, "This."

She took off his shirt and started kissing him all over his body. Moments later, Ramon was trying to make her scream his name. Nisha looked back at her ass clapping against Ramon's abdomen with great, stroke he drove into her. She took it, the pain was blissful. Holding on the headboard and the sheets for support, Nisha threw every inch of herself onto him. She was letting him know that he was hers. She was also letting him know she could take a pounding.

"Say my name," Ramon demanded.

"Daddy, it feels so good."

"Say my name," he demanded again.

"No, " Nisha said between moans of pleasure.

Nisha always did what Ramon asked her to do, but this time was different. He wanted her to scream his name. And, she was determined to hold out. The strokes only went deeper and got more intense. The sounds of her moans echoed the room along with the slapping noise of her cheeks bouncing against him.

"Say my name," Ramon requested again, holding her by her hips and her neck, penetrating her with long strokes. She moaned sexually as he thrust harder and harder.

"Say my name," he said again with authority and a little more persuasiveness. He sped up his strokes losing no stamina. Nisha snapped her neck back in pleasure as Ramon gently pulled her hair. Reaching a world of bliss, Nisha screamed, "I'm about to come for you, Daddy?"

Ramon paid no mind to her words as he kept penetrating her. The wetness sent a sensation through his body. He almost came himself, but he was focused on hearing his name. Wetness hit the sheets as Nisha moaned in a sexual release.

Ramon turned her over and slid his shaft into her as she gasped for air. He slowed down his pace as he thrusted in and out of her. Hitting her G-spot, he could tell she was loving every inch. He began to feed her long missionary strokes. Nisha's mouth opened as her back arched.

"Say my name," Ramon said, holding her legs open. Nisha's mouth quivered as she received her pleasure. Ramon felt her extending and contracting muscles. It was hypnotizing. He could sense she was about to climax again so he stroked harder and faster.

"Say my name," he demanded, gripping her checks from behind.

"Oh shit, Ramoooooon," Nisha yelled, reaching her sexual peak again.

A big smile moved to Ramon's face, leaning in to kiss her. He thrusted passionately until he felt himself about to burst. He slowed down as he reached his climax. Nisha wrapped her legs around him, grinding with him to match his tempo. Legs around him only gave him the perfect combination, an ultimate orgasm.

"Yes, Ramon," Nisha moaned, holding him tight.

Ramon released himself inside of her, filling her up with every drop.

Nisha smiled after his climax, he rolled over and took a breath.

"I shouldn't let you do that to me all the time."

Ramon laughed.

"Why?"

"Because you might get me pregnant again."

"What?" Ramon asked with a twisted face. "What do you mean, again?"

Nisha sat up and stared at him in his eyes. "Ramon, I'm pregnant."

"Are you serious?"

"Yes, I'm really pregnant. I came here to tell you and show you this."

He stared at her as she leaned over grabbing a sonogram. "This is your baby and I'm keeping his ass. So you better be a good father."

"What the fuck? You think I'm going to be a deadbeat already?"

"No," Nisha laughed.

"Good," Ramon said, putting his arms around her.

The news excited Ramon. He always wanted a child. Ramon and Nisha fell into a comfortable sleep after conversing more and another round of sex.

CHAPTER 23 – ARE YOU OKAY?

Fantasia tapped away at her laptop as she entered the dark web. She searched the latest market places, scrolling through all types of secrets. One market place supplied drugs, guns, counterfeits, company information and even organs for sale.

Fantasia minimized her screen and checked her email. She had a new email as usual. She was about to delete it when the sender's name caught her attention. It was from Simeerah Knowles.

The email read, 'Off the record, Ramon's name might be cleared. The feds found info linking Cory's murder to a police weapon. I don't really think your crew would be involved with dirty cops. I truly recommend you to inform your crew to lay low until everything clears up.'

When Fantasia finished reading, she heard a knock at her door. She grabbed her pink and chrome .380 that Ramon bought her for her 29th birthday, she yelled, "Who is it?"

"It's me," a familiar voice said.

Fantasia quickly opened the door. It was Bree with wet clothes, crying and even worse. She looked malnourished.

"Oh my God, Bree. Get in here. It's 3:30 in the morning. How did you get here and where have you been?"

"I caught an Uber."

"An Uber?" Fantasia asked, closing the door.

"Yeah."

"Where have you been?"

"Fanny, I've been in captivity."

"What? By who?"

Tears began to run down Bree's face. "By J-Dub and his fucking minions."

"Are you serious?"

"Yes," Bree said, wiping her eyes away.

"Did they touch you?"

"We can worry about that later. Where's Nisha and Ramon?"

"Are you okay?" Fantasia asked. "Are you hungry?"

"Yes, and yes, but where is Nisha and Ramon?" Bree asked again.

"They're in California."

"We have to contact them."

"Why?" Fantasia asked. "You know it's 3:45 in the morning."

"J-Dub is planning to kill them."

"What?"

"Yes, look at this," Bree said, passing Fantasia a familiar looking iPhone.

"Isn't this Jay's phone?" Fantasia asked, grabbing the phone.

"Yes, I snatched it and I kept touching it so it wouldn't go out. I used his uber account to get here. Your place was the closest place to me."

"Well, he can definitely track his phone here through the iPhone."

"Where's My iPhone app."

"I'm sorry. Everything happened so fast."

"It's okay, baby girl. I'll take care of everything."

"I'm starving."

"Go get you something to eat from the kitchen. I need to go through this iPhone and we need to do a police report."

"No," Bree said. "No cops."

"Why?"

"I think the man that kept coming to check on everything was a cop. If you read the text in his phone, it even sounds like his texting one. But he was calling him, Pop."

"What?" Fantasia asked, staring at Bree as she stuffed her face with cold leftovers. "You can sleep in the space-bedroom. We will call Nisha and Ramon in the morning. There's soap and extra towels in the bathroom. I'll bring you some spare clothes."

"Thank you, Fanny," Bree said as she walked over and gave Fantasia a long hug.

*****

"London? That's a beautiful name."

"I know," Ramon said, rolling out of the bed.

"London Dumas." Nisha said. "It's pretty."

Ramon laughed.

"What would you name it if it's a boy?"

"It would be a Junior," Nisha said as she turned to Ramon and pulled him between her legs.

"I do like that."

"I bet you wouldn't mind a little you running around that big mansion."

Ramon laughed at the ideal of a little him running around. Nisha phone rang. She reached for it and it seemed it was Fantasia.

"Why would she be calling me this early?"

Ramon smirked. "You won't find out if you don't answer."

Nisha swiped her phone. "Hello," she said, putting her phone on speaker.

"Hey, Nisha, I know it's early but we have a big problem."

"What happened, Fanny?"

"Switch to video and I'll show you?"

Nisha did what Fantasia requested.

"Okay, get ready." Fantasia said, adjusting her phone above her head. Nisha brought her phone closer to get a better view of someone sleeping. Fantasia walked to the front of her apartment and sat at her computer.

"Okay to answer your question. Yes, that is Bree. She knocked on my door at three o'clock this morning."

"I was about to ask, was that Bree?"

"Yes, she said she escaped from captivity. She also claimed that she was starved and even taken advantage of."

"Who did she say did it?"

"She says J-Dub, Rasheem, and some other guy name Pop."

"Pop?" Nisha asked as Ramon gave her a weird stare.

"Do you know someone named Pop?" Fantasia asked, staring at Nisha through Facetime."

"Not off the top of my head."

"You need to get back to Houston. We also got problems at the salon."

Nisha turned to Ramon who was nodding. "I'll be on the next flight to Houston."

"Okay, enjoy the rest of your morning, boo. I'll call you back if any new bullshit comes up or anything else pops up at my front door."

After Nisha hung up, she looked at Ramon. "I have to-"

"Trust me, I understand," Ramon said, cutting her off.

"Something's not right. I got a bad feeling when I saw Bree just laying there in Fantasia's bed. Fantasia said she-"

"I heard the conversation, boo. Just go back and I'll be back in a couple of days after you. My plane is already booked."

Minutes later, Nisha booked a last minute flight back to Houston. "You promise you'll be back in Houston in a couple of days," she asked.

"Yes, I have something that needs to be handled as soon as possible."

Nisha smiled. "Good, because you can also come to the doctor's office with me."

"Sure, I'll be at the doctor's appointment with you."

CHAPTER 24 – WHAT HAPPENED?

Rasheem woke up startled after his phone rang loud under his pillow. A number he never saw before appeared on his screen. Wanting not to answer it, he answered it anyway. "Hello"

"It's me," a familiar voice said.

"Why are you calling me from a different number?" Rasheem asked.

"Don't worry about that right now."

"What do you want then?"

"Where are you?"

"At home. Why?"

"We need to lay low. Bree escaped."

Rasheem shot up. "What!?"

"Did you tell anyone?"

"No. Did you tell Pop when she left."

"He was there when she ran off. I went to the restroom and when I came back he was laying on the ground holding his nuts."

"What the fuck?" Rasheem asked, shocked.

"I left my phone on the table and she grabbed it on her way out."

Rasheem laughed. "I bought handcuffs for situations like that."

"Everything's in that phone including info on Cory's murder."

"Why would you keep info in your phone about that?"

"Look, Lay low and just act normal until we figure everything out."

"I can do that. Do you think you and Pop can keep y'all dicks in y'all pants until then?"

"Quit with the fucking jokes. The phone is locked. It might take some time for them to get into it so we might be good."

"Have you forgotten about their geek squad bitch?"

"I'll take care of her," the familiar voice said.

"I hope so," Rasheem mumbled.

"I'll handle it."

"Do you even know where she lives?"

"Trust me, I can find out."

"Ramon moved his operation again to a hidden location, the feds are moving in, and I've recently just found out the old location has been burnt down."

"Yeah, I know about the warehouse. It has been on the news for the past two days."

"Look, this crew is ten steps ahead of us, so be careful."

"Do you think they know about us?" Rasheem asked.

"No, and we need to make sure they don't find out anything new."

"What about the phone?"

"I'll handle it."

"Cool, call me when you need me to do something."

"Believe me I will," the voice said.

"One more thing, Jay."

"What's up?"

"Be careful."

"Thanks lil bro. I will."

"Tell your mom I said hello."

"I got you," J-Dub said before hanging up.

*****

The time on Nisha's Apple Watch read 11:07 when she arrived back into Houston. Nisha raced to pick up where her friend, Vonshee was already waiting.

Half an hour later, Vonshee and Nisha were at Fantasia's apartment. Bree broke down crying and ran to Nisha and gave her a long hug. Everyone teared up. It was a long emotional six months.

"What happened?" Nisha asked, wiping Bree's tears away.

"J-Dub kidnapped me and kept me in some kind of warehouse."

"Oh my God. Did they touch you?" Vonshee asked.

Bree never answered, but her eyes told everything.

"I'm gonna kill that bastard," Vonshee said.

"Let's go inside," Fantasia suggested.

Silence filled the room after all the ladies were inside. Then Bree went into describing the events that happened to her for the past six months.

"I went home after I left Henroe's house. I went to grab some clothes. I was going back to Nisha's house. When I arrived, J-Dub was there waiting on me for some reason. He started bitching about me walking off with Henroe and dancing in front of Ramon at D-Live. I tried to ignore him, but he got angry and started hitting me. I told him I was leaving him for Henroe. Then he got furious and hit me some more. I tried to get away but he grabbed me and really forced himself on me. He was strong and I couldn't stop him."

"He fucking raped you?" Nisha asked, frowning.

"What the fuck? Hell Naw!"

"I mean technically, yes," Bree answered.

"What the fuck?" Vonshee said.

Bree dropped her head. "After everything was done. He started to cry and apologize, saying he loved me. He also said I was nobody's but his. I only belong to him."

"What?" Nisha uttered out.

"Yes, and about an hour later he fell asleep. I tried to make an escape. I made it all the way to my car and heard someone walk up behind me. They put a towel to my nose and month and whatever it was it knocked me out."

"He fucking drugged you?" Vonshee asked, staring at Bree in shock.

"Wait. How do we know it was him?" Fantasia asked.

"I don't know if it was him or not. But when I woke up in that warehouse, I smelled Jay's Gucci cologne. I was fucking scared."

"When did this guy Pop come into play?" Fantasia asked.

Bree wiped her eyes. "A little later. He wanted to know where Ramon was. I didn't understand why or even what he wanted with Ramon. Before that, J-Dub bragged about how they almost killed Nisha at her birthday celebration."

"What?" Nisha asked.

"Yes, and I also found out that Rasheem was J-Dub's half brother."

"What?" Nisha asked, raising her brow.

"I'm only assuming really because they kept talking about how families stay loyal and they kept calling each other lil bro and big bro."

"This is some bullshit," Vonshee said.

"They fed me just enough to survive. Some days I didn't even eat. And, that man Pop, kept trying to have sex with me."

"Do you remember where they kept you?" Nisha asked."

Don't worry about it, Nisha," Fantasia said. "Most likely they went into hiding by now. I tracked the location through the phone. It's in the abandoned warehouse district in Fifth Ward."

Bree nodded. "They told me they were going to make me suffer by killing Nisha. They also told me they had plans and the Pretty Divas fucked everything up."

"How did you get J-Dub's phone?" Vonshee asked.

"That man Pop showed up every other day. Yesterday I got away, Jay and Pop were there. When Jay went to the restroom, I assumed Pop thought he could come on to me and force himself on me. I made a quick decision to seduce him and try to make a dash for it. I started talking to him and dancing all sexy on him. Once I felt his little dick, I kneed him in the nuts and ran."

"You go, girl," Fantasia said.

Bree smiled. "On my way out, I seen J-Dub's phone on a table, I snatched it, and made a dash for the door.

"Did you see your phone?" Nisha asked.

"No, why?"

"Because we kept getting messages from your phone. I went to your mom's house and she said your bill was being paid," Nisha said.

Bree's face twisted. "What?"

"Yes, we all got weird texts from your phone," Fantasia said.

"I haven't had my phone since that motherfucker kidnapped me."

"We need to call Ramon," Fantasia said.

"No," Nisha said, slamming her hand on a table. "They fucked with a Pretty Diva, so Pretty Divas will handle it."

"I agree," Vonshee said.

"Well, I'm a Pretty Diva also so what do you need me to do?" Fantasia asked, turning toward Nisha.

"I need you to find out everything about J-Dub."

"You got it, Boss Lady." Fantasia said as she turned around to her computer.

"What should we do?" Vonshee asked.

"I have a plan," Nisha said, walking out of the apartment. "I'll be right back."

CHAPTER 25 - KNOWLES

Detective Knowles arrived at the station early to work on the grow house case. She called Lopez to let her know she was bringing breakfast. After she arrived and waiting in the parking lot, she was approached by Detective Black.

"Good Morning, Knowles," Black said with a slight smirk.

"Hello, Black," Knowles replied as she closed her car door .

"You headed in?"

"For a Little bit. Looks like you're headed out."

Black smiled. "You know what they say. Early bird gets the worm."

"That's what they say."

"I have something to look into."

"You need me to ride along?" Knowles asked, knowing he'll decline.

"No, I'm good."

Black jumped into his unmarked car and headed out the parking lot. Knowles sat for a moment: then, made a decision to follow him. She followed him down Austin street and onto 1-45 South. Knowles made sure to stay five cars back, but kept him in her view. After closing in, Black made a quick exit on Monroe and Edgebrook. Then pulled into Basteen Oaks, an up-scaling neighborhood with Spanish designed homes.

Moments later, Black backed his car in front of a house where he met a young man with striking resemblance of Black. Knowles packed her car at a distance, retrieving her binoculars to get a closer view. As she watched from a distance, her phone rang.

"Hello," Knowles answered.

"Where are you, partner?" Lopez asked.

"I had to make a quick stop. I'm sorry," Knowles replied.

"A quick stop?"

"Okay, I'm doing a little spying," Knowles confessed.

"On who?"

"Hmmm, no one in particular."

"So, we're keeping things from each other's partner?"

"Knowles laughed.

"Don't take it personally. I'm just nosey."

"Yeah, okay."

"If anything pans out, you'll be the first to know."

Lopez chuckled. "Yeah, yeah, so the fed lady asked if anyone found anything new on the cases."

"Not over here," Knowles said, holding the binoculars to her eyes.

"Well, I have to tell the Chief we found out that the gun was used in another murder case that also went cold."

"That's weird," Knowles said. "You want to know something weirder. I followed Black, he met up with a young man who looks just like him. Possibly a son or a younger brother."

"So, that's who you're following?"

"Yup."

"Well, if I'm correct. The young man is his oldest son, Jeremy Black Jr. Black says he's the new and improved version of him so they call him J-Dub."

"Really?"

"Yup, what's so weird about him visiting his son?"

"I guess nothing," Knowles said, starting her car and driving off.

"Well, hurry back when you're done. We have leads to follow."

"I will," Knowles said, doing one final glance in her mirror.

*****

As Detective Black conversed with his son, he thought he saw an unmarked police car. But he thought nothing of it.

"Why did you want to meet here?" J-Dub asked.

"Home is always the safest place to be, boy," Black responded.

"What are we going to do about this Bree situation?"

"That whole crew needs to go down."

"How did you let that bitch seduce you? Now, look at us."

"Watch your mouth, boy."

"I'm just saying, Pop," J-Dub said, shaking his head.

"You should have done your part months ago. Take out Cory then Ramon. Then we would've had the whole operation by now. I gave you a place to take care for everything. And I gave you a throw away gun that came from an ex-cop."

"I know, but these Pretty Diva bitches fucking everything up. Charles beat his case on a tech."

"I know that, boy."

"I also have something to tell you.

Black puffed. "What is it?"

"Bree took my phone the night she escaped."

"What!?" Black said with a wrath.

"I had to get another one. I'm sorry, Pop. I knew you were in a lot of pain that night so I never brought it up."

"You need to get that phone back! Everything is on that phone! All the connections between us and everyone in that department is in that phone."

"I know, " J-Dub said, dropping his head.

"What the fuck?" Black said, putting his hands on his head.

"I still have Bree's phone. I can send a text to them and try to lure them out."

"No, give me the phone. I'll handle everything. I've already been covering up your mess. I don't need anything else fucked up. Just lay low until I call and tell your brother to do the same. Just act normal."

"What will you do?"

"Let's just say, they can rest in peace with their little ol' Cory."

Black's work phone rang. "Hold on, I have to take this." Black listened with a straight face. Then he told his caller he'll handle it and hung up.

"Everything's okay?" J-Dub asked.

"Yes. I have to head back to the Hall. I'll set up everything and call you later. And tell your mother I said Hello.

"You're closer to her than I am," J-Dub laughed as Black jumped in his car and pulled away."

*****

Detective Knowles was back at the Hall with a cold McDonald's. She dropped Lopez's bag of food on her desk and sat next to her.

"How was the trip?" Lopez asked, reaching inside her bag.

"Wasn't bad. Nice house though. Spanish style. You would have loved it. Knowles said with a giggle."

"So, you got jokes?" Lopez laughed.

"Well, I will try."

"Chief wants us to bring new info to her. I was going to bring this to her but, I wanted to wait for you to get back. It came in right after we got off the phone. It's addressed to you. They delivered it to me because you were out. I couldn't help myself. I peaked in it. It's from a private sender."

"That's a federal offense, Detective."

Lopez smiled. "Take me to jail."

Knowles re-opened the manilla envelope and pulled out the photos.

Knowles gasped, putting her hand over her mouth. "What the hell?"

Lopez took a bit out of her cold McGriddle. "Exactly why I wanted to wait on you to see it first. Now, you really think she'll like this?"

Knowles leaned back in her chair. "I don't think we should show her this. Not yet."

187

"I agree," Lopez said, taking a sip of her orange juice.

CHAPTER 26 - HEAVEN

Rasheem thought he was dreaming, hearing knocks at his door. He glanced at his watch. It was eight in the morning. He huffed then dropped his head back into his pillow after a louder knock. He threw off his covers, stormed to the door and snatched it open. It was only Charles in a black hoodie, black Jordans and a pair of black 501 jeans.

"Damn, Bro, you okay?" Charles asked, stepping back.

"Yeah, my fault, I was asleep."

"Naw, it's my fault."

"No, it's okay," Rasheem said, motioning Charles in.

"What's up?" Charles asked, stepping inside and closing the door.

"You tell me. Is Ramon ready to start operations back up?"

"Yeah, he got plans but you know we moving on his time."

"Well, what brings you to my domain?" Rasheem asked as he sat down on his couch.

"You know he ain't doing shit but, I still got some weed and pills. I want you to ride along with me to do a drop. I really don't trust this dude."

"Me? Why didn't you ask Nisha or Vonshee?" Rasheem laughed.

"I'm not about to take any females with me. You know that."

"Okay, why not take J-Dub?"

Charles titled his head. "You sure are asking a lot of questions."

Rasheem smiled. "Sorry, it's just a habit."

"I had to pass your place so I stopped by and asked. We really don't like chilling so I thought I would invite you. If you don't want to roll, it's cool."

"I'll just ride by myself," Charles said.

"What's in it for me?" Rasheem asked as he lit a Newport.

Charles laughed. "Ha, you're always on some scheming shit. I'll cut you in on the drop. But we have to leave now if you're going. We need to meet him in one hour."

The music made time fly by as Charles and Rasheem pulled into an area that the city knew well but no one would ever be caught there. 'No Man's Land.'

Charles lit a marijuana joint he had rolled before the trip.

"Damn, that smells good. What is it?" Rasheem asked.

"It's a new strain Ramon and I put together. We call it Double Haze."

Rasheem laughed. "Why y'all call it that?"

"I think because it give you two different highs while you're smoking it. But then again, you'll have to ask Ramon himself."

"Let me hit it. I'll tell you know if it's true or not," Rasheem said, smiling with his fingers out.

"Sure," Charles said, passing him the joint.

Rasheem took to puffs and blew smoke out. He inhaled another puff, held it, and released another cloud of smoke. "It is some good shit."

"I told you," Charles said.

"Where your guy at?'" Rasheem asked in a relaxed voice.

"He'll be here," Charles said as he fired up another joint.

"Where are we?"

Charles smirked. "This is No Man's Land?"

"What? Why would anyone want to meet here?"

"I thought the same thing."

"Crazy place to meet up for a quick drug transaction." Rasheem, laughed lightly.

"I have a question for you, Rasheem."

"Shoot."

"How long have you admired my girlfriend?"

Rasheem eyes widen as he gave a nervous laugh. "What the hell? What kind of question is that?"

"How long have you've admired Vonshee? Be honest," Charles said, hitting just joint.

"What kind of question is that?" Rasheem asked as he put his joint out.

"Be real with me. I've seen how you look at her. I just want to know if I can trust you around my girl," Charles said, blowing smoke from his nose.

"Yeah, I think she's pretty. But I would never disrespect you and her relationship."

Charles looked down at his phone and replied to a text. He opened the car door and stepped out. "He's around the corner."

"Cool," Rasheem replied as he stepped out to join Charles.

"I really do believe you, Rasheem. But, I have another question for you. And be honest with me answering this question as you did the first."

Rasheem smiled awkwardly. "Just call me, Honest Joe."

Charles pulled out a chrome Beretta from under his seat. "How long have you been a snitch bitch who burns down a operation that help, put money in your pockets?" he said, closing the door.

Rasheem eyed the Beretta.

"What are you doing, Charles?"

"I'm waiting for you to answer my question." Charles pointed the gun at Rasheem's forehead.

"What are you talking about?" Rasheem cried.

"Oh, you wanna play?" Charles dialed Ramon's number. Once Ramon was on the phone, he hit the speaker button and threw Rasheem the phone.

"Rasheem, my man," Ramon said through the speaker. "What have you been up to?"

Silence was the only response Rasheem could give.

Ramon laughed. "Well, since you don't remember, I'll remind you. You've been lying, stealing, cheating and snitching, You've also let your lust for Vonshee get the best of you. See me, I always stay ten steps ahead of the next man. Especially men like you. See, my warehouse is bugged and has installed hidden cameras so I know everything that's done and talked about. You made a call to your father and got Charles arrested. Your brother J-Dub has been no better with that envy shit he has for me. Y'all even planned to kill my girl. You also became a C.I. for your father and other cops and that's fucked up. Disloyalty plays no part in this organization. So, we took a vote to send you to your maker."

The phone went silent and Rasheem stood there shocked.

"You're done with that phone call, buddy?" Charles asked as he raised the Beretta to Rasheem's face again.

The iPhone hit the concrete.

"Are you fucking serious?" Charles said. "You're going to pay for that. Now pick it up and give it to me."

Rasheem followed the order. "Please don't shoot me," Rasheem begged as he handed Charles's phone back to him.

"You must have thought we weren't going to find out about y'all?"

"You don't understand. My Dad made me do it. It was all his and J-Dub's plan. I just wanted them to accept me. I just got back in contact with them. They said if I wanted to be apart of their family, then I had to do it. I did it because I wanted them to love me."

Charles stepped closer, still aiming at Rasheem's head. "Where's your brother?"

"You know I can't tell you that. He'll kill me."

Charles shook his head looking at his gun. "Are you serious right now?"

"Please don't kill me. I'll tell you what really happened to Cory

"What?" Charles asked, tilting his head.

Rasheem repeated.

"So you know who killed Cory?"

"I mean...."

Charles dialed Ramon's number.

"It's good?" Ramon asked, after the pick up.

"Naw, I think you need to hear this funny as shit." Charles said, putting the phone on speaker and demanding Rasheem to speak.

"If you let me live, I'll tell you what happened to Cory," Rasheem said.

"I think you didn't hear me good the first time we spoke. Remember I told you I stay ten steps ahead of the next man. I already know what happened to Cory."

"Ramon, please," Rasheem cried out.

The phone hung up, shock and confusion crept into Rasheem's face.

BANG, BANG!

Charles planted two bullets right in the middle of Rasheem's forehead.

The gun sound echoed through the air. Then there was a quick silence after his body hit the ground. Charles stared at Rasheen's Lifeless body and nodded in approval. He thoroughly cleaned the gun off and placed it in the dead man's hand.

After smoking another joint, Charles calmly climbed back into his car and drove off, leaving Rasheem staring at the heavens.

"Is it done?" Ramon asked after answering Charles' phone call.

"Done like a well-cooked steak."

*****

Nisha woke up to the sound of her phone's ringtone. When she looked over, she saw Fantasia's name flashing. She quickly reached over and answered. She'd been expected news about J-Dub's location.

"Hello," Nisha yawned out.

"You sound sleepy?"

"I'm up."

"Well, I spent the whole night cracking J-Dub's phone. He has some weird shit in here."

Nisha laughed. "What, like porn?"

"Yeah, but the messages in here seem like he's been talking to a cop."

"A Cop? Jay? All the bullshit he's into. Are you sure about that?"

"Seems that way and it's programmed under Pop. But I think Pop is his nickname. I think he calls him Pop because it's his father."

"Are you serious? You think he had his dad involved?"

"Yes."

"That's crazy," Nisha said. "What else did you find?"

"A couple of bitches and an interesting thread with Rasheem."

"Well, they were close. Have you seen him lately?"

"No, I haven't. And they were close, like family close."

Nisha was raised in her bed. "What do you mean by that?"

"In the thread he and Rasheem are talking about Pop. J-Dub mentions their father leaving his mother for Rashee's mother. They poked fun at the whole thing."

"Yup, I also did some more hacking and found a contract between Verizon and J-Dub. The contract gave me J-Dub's real name."

Switching the phone from one ear to the next, Nisha asked. "Isn't his name Jeremy."

"Yes, his name is Jeremy Rogelio Black, Jr."

"Okay, does that mean anything?" Nisha asked, putting her slippers on.

"It could. I did some more digging and I found out the detective who was over your brother's case was named Jeremy Rogelio Black, Sr."

"What the hell?" Nisha gasped.

"Yes, J-Dub's father is a cop and he was over your brother's case until it with cold last year. He's also over the parking lot shooting case from your birthday."

Nisha was in shock, holding the phone with her mouth wide.

"And, guess what else?" Fantasia asked.

"What?" Nisha asked as her mind raced with a million thoughts.

"J-Dub recently made some calls."

"Hmm, so he purchased another phone?" Nisha said. "This shit is crazy. I need to call Ramon and tell him everything."

"Yeah, you do that. I'll call you when I get some more information."

Nisha hung up as she got out of bed. She got dressed and headed out the door.

CHAPTER 27 – SHIT IT DOWN

Bree woke up from a peaceful sleep when Nisha returned with breakfast. Bree knew Nisha was worried about her. She was pale, fragile, starved and beaten. Bree was disgusted by the events that had happened to her so she truly understood her friend's concern.

"I brought you breakfast, Bree," Nisha said, walking toward the bed.

"Thanks, but you didn't have to get me nothing," Bree replied.

Nisha laughed as Bree snatched the bag.

"You say that, but you snatched that bag like it was going somewhere."

"I never said I wasn't hungry."

"What are you doing today?"

"I don't know," Bree answered, taking a big bite out of her breakfast.

"What about you? Do you have anything special planned for today?"

Nisha looked up at the ceiling. "I might have something special planned for a special someone."

"Who, Ramon?"

Looking into the corner of her eyes, Nisha laughed. "Ramon don't really deserve this."

Bree stared at Nisha. "What's that supposed to mean?"

"Nothing, but eat and get ready. I'm dropping you off at the salon today. I'll meet you back at the mansion. You can just take an Uber back."

"Whatever you say, Boss Lady," Bree said, stuffing her face with the rest of her breakfast sandwich and heading to the bathroom.

"I see your booty didn't go anywhere," Nisha said, joking as Bree twisted away toward the bathroom.

Bree giggled and twerked with her tongue out.

"I know, all forty inches is still here."

"Forty inches?" Girl please."

*****

Nisha dialed Selena's number on her way down stairs. Nisha needed a way to get close to J-Dub. She needed someone he didn't know and Selena was the perfect candidate.

"*Hola, Mami*," Selena answered in her sexy Puerto Rican voice.

"Hey, Bonita. Are you off today?"

"*Si, por que?*"

"Because, I need you to do me a favor."

"Okay, let me hear it."

Nisha paused. "I need you to buy some coke from someone."

"Are you serious?" Selena asked surprised.

"Yes, I need you to place an order for some coke. I need to lure someone out of hiding. I need this little boy to come out and play. I'm calling him a little boy because of what he did to my friend. Real men don't hit women. He loves to sell coke so I know this will work."

"Okay, explain it to me a little bit more, *Mami*."

"You will text him asking for some coke. Most likely he'll give you a location to meet you to do the transaction. He might ask where he even met you at? Tell him you're a friend of Diamond. That's his side chick from D-Live. Send him a picture even if he doesn't ask for one. You're super beautiful so, he'll agree to meet you. Once that's established, I'll explain more to you."

"Okay, sounds simple. I can do that for you, *Mami!*"

Nisha smiled. "Good, but first we need to go and get you a burner phone from the dollar store. And, I must warn you-"

"Stop it. I'm a Puerto Rican from the streets of New York. I know how to handle myself."

"Well, excuse me missy. I'll pick you up in a little bit, so be ready."

"Yes, *Mamacita.*"

After Nisha hung up, she turned around and noticed Bree staring at her. "What?" Nisha asked with a slight smirk.

"What are you up to, Nisha?" Bree asked, drying herself with a towel.

"Nothing."

Bree pointed her finger. "No, I know you, Nisha. What are you doing?"

"I'm just going to pay your ex-boyfriend a little visit. That's all."

"Well, I heard everything and I want to go with y'all."

"I don't think that's a good idea," Nisha stated, folding her arms.

"You're almost a month pregnant and you're telling me what you think a good idea is? Are you fucking serious?"

"Okay," Nisha said, "but I just don't want you there if something bad were to happen."

"Nisha, look at what these motherfuckers did to me. Look at my face, look at my weight, look at these bruises. I want to go with y'all."

Nisha frowned then gave in. "Alright, but if things get bad, I need you to leave."

Bree nodded. "Okay."

Nisha stared at all the bruises on Bree as Bree turned and walked away.

The sight of them made her want to vomit.

"Did you hear me?" Bree asked.

Nisha snapped back from her thoughts. "I'm sorry, I was thinking about something. What did you say, Bree?"

"I said let me get ready so we can go and pick up your *mamacita*."

Nisha smiled. "Okay, and I have to call Vonshee and tell her we're coming to pick her up also."

CHAPTER 28 – SELENA

Ramon enjoyed the view of the city as the plane landed at Bush Intercontinental Airport. After retrieving all of his luggage at the busy terminal, he made his way to pick-up where Charles was waiting. Ramon threw his belongings into the backseat of Charles's Lexus, jumped into the front seat, and they sped off into the city of Houston.

"Charles, what it do?" Ramon asked Charles as he stopped at the first stop light.

"Same as everyday. Out here trying to make some more money."

"Cool, cool, cool," Ramon responded.

"Where are you trying to go?" Charles asked, pressing the gas pedal as the light turned green.

Ramon twisted his lips while tilting his head.

"Take me to the mansion."

"I got you. After that, we can slide by the new locations of the operation. We got it hooked up pretty nicely."

"Yeah, we can do that. Make sure to tell no one that I'm back in town," Ramon's demanded.

Charles laughed. "Why would I do that?"

"Stop by a Jack-N-The Box. I'm hungry as hell."

"Shit, me too."

"Have you seen J-Dub?" Ramon asked. "I heard he's been missing in action since the Bree situation."

"Naw, do we need to be looking for him?" Charles asked.

Ramon swiped at his phone.

"Yes and no. Fantasia did some of her digging and found some very interesting information. You know Fanny, a beast with that tech shit. She's been riding with me since day one."

"Yeah I know."

"So, look at this," Ramon said, handing Charles his iPhone.

"What the hell?"

"That's the same thing I said when I saw it."

Charles studied the photo a little longer after stopping at a light.

"Wait a minute," Charles said. "That's J-Dub, Rasheem and the guy next to him looks just like Rasheem. But who's the chick?"

Ramon grabbed his phone from Charles and scrolled through it and found another picture. "Yes, now look at this. This is father and son. J-Dub's family tree. Rasheem twin brother is named Kareem and the chick looks familiar but I don't know who she is.

"This is crazy."

"Yup, and you know Detective Black, who arrested you. But look at this."

"What the fuck?" Charles asked, doing a quick glance.

Ramon grinned.

"This is J-Dub's birth certificate. Look at the names of the father and son."

"Jeremy Rogelio Black, Sr. and Jeremy Rogelio Black, Jr. What the hell? J-Dub must be his way of saying he's number two."

"Bingo," Ramon replied.

"This is some wild shit. Rasheem was a twin?"

"Told you Fantasia was a beast. I don't even know how she got this birth certificate."

Charles laughed, turning into a Jack-N-The Box parking lot. "Well, she is a badass hacker. So we do know where Rasheem is, I left him staring at the sky in No Man's Land. So, where's his brother and mother?"

"I'm glad you asked. Rasheem's brother is no longer known by Kareem. He goes by the name Karmen now. And she is a big time advocate for the LBGTQ community. I had Fanny track her down. Let's just say they had a very interesting conversation."

"What!?" Charles asked, putting the Lexus into park.

"Look at this," Ramon said, handing his phone back to Charles.

Charles looked at the photo on the phone. "Who is this?"

"That my friend is Karmen."

"What?" Charles said with an arched eyebrow.

"Yeah," Ramon laughed. "And I won't tell anyone about that curious look you just had on your face when you seen this picture."

"What look?" Charles asked as Ramon grabbed his phone.

"Anyways. I think Karmen was neglected as a child because Fanny said she hasn't talked to the Blacks in years. Fantasia said once she revealed herself."

"They didn't take the news very well, especially her older sister. We think jealousy comes into play. Fantasia said the sister went and got surgery for more beauty and enhancements. Said she was determined to look like someone famous."

"So, now what?" Charles asked.

"We go order and head to the mansion. I feel like pushing the Challenger today. You can follow if you want or you can ride."

"Riding," Charles said, stepping out of the car.

"Cool, I want to surprise Nisha with my early arrival."

Selena called J-Dub multiple times before he answered. She could tell by his tone of voice that he was on edge.

"Who is this?" J-Dub answered, after picking up.

"Can I speak to J-Dub?" Selena asked putting her phone on speaker for everyone in the car to hear. I'm Selena and I was calling to buy some coke."

"I don't know no one named Selena."

"Well, I know you," she said in a Spanish accent.

"Diamond gave me your number. She said I could call you if I needed a hook up. I saw you at D-Live. So, I always knew who you were."

J-Dub laughed. "You dance at D-Live?"

"Sometimes."

"Well, I don't remember you. So, send me a picture."

Selena and Nisha fist bumped with a smile.

"Are you serious?" Selena said into the phone with a slight hesitation.

"Yes, I like to know who I'm dealing with," J-Dub answered.

"Okay, I'm sending it to you right now, *papi*."

The call went silent for a moment. "Hmm, I guess I can sell to your sexy self. I never saw you in D-Live. But, you are so bad, I know you dance there."

"You've been so focused on other *putas*. I guess you missed me."

"I guess so. So you want some coke?" J-Dub asked.

Selena turned to Nisha holding the phone. "No, I need coke. Especially when I get horny."

"Is that right?"

"*Si*, papi," Selena said in a sexy Latina voice.

"How much are you trying to get?"

Selena paused. "A quarter?"

"Damn, what are you gonna do with all of that?"

"I sell a little bit, *tambien, papi.*"

"I guess. Well, I'm about to ping you my location. Just pull up and call me when you're outside."

"Okay. Can you do me a favor?" Selena asked.

"What's up, sexy?"

"Please don't tell Diamond that I'm coming through. I want to keep whatever we do a secret, *papi*."

"Yeah, I can do that for you," J-Dub replied.

"*Adios, papi!* I'll call you when I'm there. I hope you ready for all of this," Selena giggled before hanging up.

"Huh, ready for what?"

Selena ended the call. "OMG. That went a lot smoother than I thought."

"I know, right?" Nisha sneakered.

"Did he send the ping?" Bree asked, typing away at her phone.

"Yup, he just sent it, " Selena answered.

"Who are you texting, Bree?" Nisha asked, adjusting her rearview mirror.

Bree smiled and looked up. "Henroe."

"You can't be serious? Nisha asked. "Let's go visit your ex."

Nisha pulled up to a red light and glanced at all of her friends. Selena heard so much about Bree. Nisha had always talked about her high school friend and always said she was one tough cookie. Selena turned away from Nisha then looked out the window. She remembered one night visiting Nisha, she told her a story about how they had become friends and cheerleaders together. Bree had really always gotten into arguments with other girls. Not wanting to get in trouble at school, everyone would always meet and fight at Anderson Park down the street. Nisha heard about other fights, but only seen three and little Bree was victorious in all bouts.

*****

After the pinged address was given and setting everything up, Selena knocked on the door. J-Dub answered, wearing a muscle shirt, house slippers, and a pair of basketball shorts.

"Come in," J-Dub said, waving his hands.

Selena stepped in wearing a skin tight dress that exposed all of her curves. "This is a nice place," she said.

"Thanks beautiful. What can I do for you?"

Selena giggled.

"Papi, we already talked about this."

"Right." J-Dub said with a laugh. "Well, follow me."

Selena followed, admiring the expensive taste of his home.

"So, you live here by yourself?"

"I do now."

"Why do you say it like that, *papi*?"

J-Dub walked into a room that Selena could only assume was a home studio for recording. "This is where I keep my supplies and you can say my last bitch didn't make it. Let's just say she ran away from the relationship."

"Really?" Selena asked with a slight smile.

"Yup. Take a seat on the sofa, I got something for you and I got your dope ready," J-Dub said.

"Okay, I'm lying. I have to go and back it up."

Selena laughed. "It's ready, isn't it?"

"Naw, not yet. I got busy doing something else."

J-Dub opened a closet show-casing ten bricks of cocaine."

Selena's eyes grew wide.

"Yeah, I know," J-Dub said, nodding his head slowly.

Selena examined the room as J-Dub bagged her order. "Did you draw that?" she asked, pointing at an art picture of Tupac.

"Yeah, I draw in my space time," J-Dub answered, weighing the product.

"Was that your Challenger outside?"

J-Dub laughed with a crooked smile. "Yeah, this hoe ass nigga named Ramon put me on them. Then he goes and gets one that's just like mines. I don't know why, maybe he wanted to be Like me or something.

"*De Veras?*" Selena asked, smiling, even though she knew the truth.

"What does that mean?"

"It means For Real?"

"Here you go," J-Dub said, giving Selena her packed product.

"Thank you. Let me get your money and send a text to my homegirl to tell her I'm on my way."

Selena texted away at her phone, then reached into her Gucci purse, pulled out a roll of money and paid J-Dub his payment. "It was a pleasure."

"No, it was my pleasure," J-Dub said, thumbing through the roll of cash.

"Well, I'll see ya later, *papi*."

"Sit down for a minute, let's party," J-Dub said, grabbing Selena's arm.

"No, I'm okay. I just wanted to buy and leave."

"Come one. You come all this way to see me and you don't want to have no fun?"

"What do you mean by fun?" Selena asked.

J-Dub reached for a trey with two lines of coke on it and a rolled hundred dollar bill. "You say you need coke when you're horny."

"Yeah, but."

"But what?" J-Dub asked, then sniffed a line.

"No, that's okay. I really have to go."

"You're just going to leave like that?" J-Dub asked, standing in front of Selena.

"Yeah, I have to go."

J-Dub pushed Selena down as she stood up. "Let's play," he said, putting himself between her legs and leaning in for a kiss.

"No, I'm good."

"Damn girl," J-Dub said as Selena pulled away.

"I said I have to go," Selena yelled as she slapped him.

"What the fuck is wrong with you, bitch?" J-Dub asked, grabbing his face.

"I have to go."

J-Dub pushed Selena again causing her to hit the sofa.

"You got me fucked up," he said, reaching his hands up her skirt. "You tell me don't tell Diamond, then come way over here acting like you want some, and you think you just going to leave without out giving me some? You got me fucked up."

"Stop," Selena yelled, trying harder to get away.

"Bitch, you're gonna give me some of this Spanish pussy."

J-Dub tried to put his weight on top of Selena but came to a sudden stop as he felt a cold metal barrel to his temple.

"I'll advise you to do what my friend asked and get the fuck off of her,"

Nisha said, smiling at Selena. "You okay, Mamacita?"

Selena smiled back. "Yup, it went just as you planned."

Nisha pushed the barrel to his head. "Get the fuck up, slowly."

J-Dub put his hands up and slowly stood to his feet. "What the fuck you doing in my house?"

Nisha laughed. "Why don't you take a seat and I'll tell you."

Selena stood up, adjusted her dress and smiled at J-Dub. "It was nice meeting you, papi."

As J-Dub took his seat, he seen Bree and Vonshee standing behind Nisha. Both women were also holding their own personal weapons.

"You know you should learn to lock your doors, Jeremy," Bree joked.

"What do you hoes want?" J-Dub asked.

"Hoes? Try, Pretty Divas," Vonshee said.

"You thought you and your crew could just rape and beat my homegirl and get away with it?" Nisha asked.

"I ain't rape nobody," J-Dub shot back, glancing at Bree. Nisha stuck her .380 Semi-Auto into J-Dub's crotch.

Everyone's eyes widened.

"What the fuck?" J-Dub asked, flinching.

Bree laughed. "Oh snap, he's scared now."

"Scared? Bitch who wouldn't be. But this bitch doesn't have the balls. If she shoots me, that'll be her ass. My father's a cop and she'll be locked up for years. So, she can take her chances if she wants."

"We already know about your Pop," Nisha laughed.

"Yeah, but he's right, Nisha," Bree said.

J-Dub smiled. "Yeah, listen to your bitch. You bitches run around here thinking y'all cute with that Pretty Diva shit. Nisha, you'll never be like your brother. And when Ramon's done using you up, you'll be right back to the hood. I gave Cory my all and you know what he gave me in return? A spit to the face. I left to the army, and came back to Cory and Ramon having a weed operation and they were millionaires. After all he and I had been through, he became close with Ramon."

Nisha frowned. "So, you did all of this because you were jealous of Cory and Ramon's friendship."

"Ha, this was more about power!" J-Dub said.

"Power?" Vonshee asked.

"I tried to make the operation bigger and better. I tried to bring in the coke, which could have been greater money. But Cory said no only because Ramon didn't want to be a part of the coke business. My father would have protected us and kept the feds away. He would have kept us safe from law enforcement. All we had to do was cut him in on profits. They denied our offer. My brother and I came up with a plan to get rid of the double headed monster. But we needed my father's help. And he loved the idea."

"What idea?" Nisha asked, pushing the .380 into J-Dub's privates causing him to flinch again.

"The idea was to take out Ramon first then Cory. But a disagreement changed all of that."

"What?" Bree asked.

"Oh my God, he got into it with Cory and shot him," Selena said.

BANG! The sound of Nisha's gun echoed in the room.

"Oh shit." Bree screamed.

"Aww, hell naw, bitch I'm gonna kill you," J-Dub said as he fell to the floor, holding himself.

Blood from J-Dub's thigh started to leak through his hands and drip to the floor. Vonshee grabbed Nisha's hand. "Let's go, Nisha, we have to leave. I know someone heard that."

"Uggghhh," J-Dub moaned.

"You dirty bitches."

"We need to go, Mami," Selena said, putting her hands on Nisha's shoulder and unwrapping Nisha's fingers from around her pistol.

"I'ma kill you, bitch," J-Dub yelled again as the ladies rushed out. J-Dub tried to stand and chase, but only went stumbling down in pain from the gunshot wound.

The Pretty Divas exited the building and jumped into Nisha's Impala. Nisha started the car and sped off, burning rubber.

"Oh my God, you just shot J-Dub in the nuts," Bree said, seeming like she could wait to get it out.

"What the fuck are we about to do? Where are we about to go?" Vonshee asked, putting her gun in her purse.

"I'm going to kill that motherfucker. He killed Cory," Nisha said.

"We don't know that for sure, Nisha," Vonshee said.

"Yeah, he really didn't say it, Nisha," Bree added.

"*Mira, mi amor,* no one knows where I live. So, go to my house, Nisha," Selena said from the backseat.

"That's a great idea," Nisha said as she ran a red light.

CHAPTER 29 – RIDE OR DIE

Music blasted through Ramon's Hellcat's speaker. It felt good to be back in the city. He loved everything about Houston from the streets, the music, all the way to the culture.

"I have big plans for us," Ramon said to Charles, who was listening to Bun B, and watching a Chevy Impala zoom through the red light.

"What the hell?" Charles said. "That car could've caused a wreck."

Ramon studied the vehicle as it sped by. Intuition told him to look at the car's license plate. "Oh shit! That's Nisha."

"How do you know?" Charles asked, turning the music down.

"I think I know my girlfriend's car when I see it. Plus, I know her plate number. But that's her for sure."

"What the hell is she doing on this side of town?" Charles questioned.

Ramon shrugged. "Probably doing a drop, but why is she speedy?"

"I wonder if Vonshee's with her?" Charles asked. "I'ma call her."

"Naw, don't worry about it. I'm going to follow her," Ramon said as the light turned green.

*****

Nisha's mind raced as she drove down Broadway, making a left on Bellfort. The trip to Selena's was a hard silence and no one really wanted to break it. Nisha looked at her friends in her rearview mirror and was lost for words.

"Are you mad at me, Bree?" Nisha finally asked.

"Why would I be mad at you?"

"For what I did to your ex-boyfriend."

"For what they did to me they deserve to be put six feet deep."

"I agree," Vonshee said.

"Oh my God," Selena said, looking behind her.

"What is it?" Nisha asked.

"Isn't this J-Dub behind us?"

Nisha looked in the rearview mirror. "This motherfucker."

"He's been following us the whole time," Vonshee stated.

Bree turned around and watched the Challenger follow. "I know a street no one really goes down. At the next light make a right and then make a quick left on Pampa Street."

"What do you want to do, Bree?" Nisha asked.

"If he follows us down the street, I'm going to get out and light his car up."

"You know what, Bree? I'm with you," Vonshee said.

Nisha stared at her friends and smiled. It felt good to have a group of girls that had her back through thick and thin. Nisha turned down Pampa Street driving slowly. The street was dark and gloomy with trees that hung over. Moments later, the red Challenger turned down the street. Nisha quickly threw her Impala into park.

"Oh shit, here we go," Bree said.

Without hesitation all four women exited the vehicle, pointed their guns and opened fire. The Challenger came to a complete stop and took every raving bullet.

The windshield rapidly cracked from impact along with the headlights.

All four women jumped back into the car as Nisha threw the car back into drive and mashed the gas, leaving the Challenger sitting.

*****

Alter bullets stopped flying through the window, Charles raised his head and seen Ramon's body struggling to move.

"What the fuck?" Charles yelled as he quickly exited the passenger side and eased to Ramon's side. He checked Ramon's pulse and felt a beat. Ramon's eyes brought fear to Charles as he pulled him out of the delver's seat and moved him fast to the back. Knowing where the closest hospital was, he leaped into the front seat and rushed Ramon to the hospital.

"Stay with me," Charles yelled from the front seat.

"We're almost there."

Minutes later, Charles pulled into Southeast Memorial Hospital, "Help!" he yelled out the window.

Two nurses who seemed to be taking a break was standing outside of the emergency room.

A nurse rushed over. "Oh my God," the blonde nurse said. "Go get a gurney,"

The second nurse went and retrieved a gurney. "What happened?" the second nurse asked when she returned.

"He was shot?" Charles said.

Seconds later, more nurses appeared.

"He's going to need surgery," one nurse said.

"Get him upstairs now."

"What's his name?" the nurse asked as they transferred Ramon to the hospital,

"Ramon," Charles said,

The blonde nurse shone a light in Ramon's eyes. "Okay, Mr. Ramon, I'm Ashley Hillton. We're going to help you."

Ramon's eyes were dazed, glazed and filled with pain. Charles followed the nurse to the operation room but was stopped.

"I'm sorry, Mr.?"

"Lyons," Charles said.

"I'm sorry, Mr. Lyons, but you're not allowed back here. Please go to the waiting room. We'll do all we can to save him."

"Please save him, Ms. Hillton."

"We will, but I need you to calm down and have a seat in the waiting room so we can do our job."

Realizing he left the car parked in front of the emergency room, Charles raced back to the Challenger. When he got into Ramon's Hellcat, he saw his phone. Not thinking clearly, he phoned Vonshee but hung up. He needed to move the car first.

*****

Nisha finally made it to Selena's neighborhood. Nisha's heart raced and she wondered if the other's hearts were pounding like hers.

"I can't believe he tried to follow us," Bree said.

"I can't believe we just shot up his car," Vonshee said.

"I can't believe Nisha shot him in the *juevos*," Selena slightly laughed.

"I couldn't help it. The gun just went off. Did you hear what he said about Cory? He let his brother and father touch Bree. It just happened."

"That was a nice car, too. I like that car," Bree said.

"Well, I don't, it looks too much like Ramon's car."

Nisha pulled into the driveway of Selena's house. She glanced at Vonshee, who was staring out the window. Vonshee turned to Nisha. "What?" Vonshee asked.

"Are you okay?" Nisha asked.

Vonshee looked down. "Yeah, I know this is bad timing. But I'm just thinking. Charles told me something bad happened to Rasheem. Then we do this to J-Dub. It's just a lot to take in."

"Well."

Nisha was cut off by the ringing of Vonshee's phone.

Vonshee looked at the caller and answered. "Hello."

Vonshee listened as the caller yelled. "Are you kidding me?" she cried.

Nisha and the others stared at her, probably wondering what brought her to tears so quickly.

"No. She's my friend so I'll tell her," Vonshee said into the phone.

Everyone's eyes were on her as she ended the call.

"What's wrong, Vonshee?" Nisha asked.

"Yeah, what's wrong? Selena added.

Vonshee's eyes dropped. "I'm so sorry, Nisha."

"Sorry? For what?" Nisha asked.

Vonshee wiped her eyes.

"Long story short. We didn't shoot at J-Dub, we shot at Ramon and Charles."

"What?" Nisha roared. "Are you fucking serious? Where the hell is Ramon?"

"Charles said they're at Southeast Memorial and Ramon is in surgery."

Nisha had no response as she quickly threw the car in reverse, backed out the driveway, slammed the car in drive and shot out of the neighborhood as tears rushed down her face.

Twenty minutes later they arrived at the hospital. The Pretty Divas raced into the hospital. They reached the information desk where they were met by a beautiful redhead.

"How can I help you ladies?" the redhead asked.

"We're looking for Ramon Dumas," Nisha said with a cracked voice.

"Okay," the redhead responded as she typed away at her computer. "Mr. Dumas just got out of surgery. He's in the ICU upstairs, fifth floor."

"Thank you," Nisha said as she ran to the elevator.

"I'm texting Charles," Vonshee said, "I'm telling him we're headed up there."

Once the women reached the floor, Charles and a nurse were engaging in a conversation.

"Where is he, Charles?" Nisha asked, crying.

Charles turned to Nisha and the Divas. "He's in room 346. But before you go, I really think you need to talk to the nurse. This is Nurse Ashley Hillton."

The nurse extended her hand. "Hello, I'm Nurse Hillton.

Nisha shook her hand. "I'm Nisha, Ramon's girlfriend."

"Ms. Nisha, your boyfriend was severely shot multiple times. A bullet did pierce his lung, we pulled a bullet fragment from his core and his shoulder. He also had a bullet graze his skull."

"Oh my God," Nisha said, putting her hands over her mouth.

"You can see him, but I must warn you, we did everything we could do to save him."

"Okay, so what's the problem?" Selena asked.

"Mr. Dumas can't speak," the nurse answered after a short paused.

"What do you mean he can't speak?" Nisha asked, eyeing the nurse.

"Mr. Dumas is in a coma and we can't say when he will wake up."

"Are you serious?" Nisha asked, looking at Charles.

"Yes, and since he was involved in a shooting, by law, the hospital had to inform the police."

"Fuck that, can I just see him," Nisha asked, crying.

"Yes, ma'am. If you need anything, please feel free to buzz me."

*****

Nisha led the pack as everyone entered Ramon's room. As soon as she laid eyes on him, she ran to the bed in tears.

"I'm so sorry, Baby," Nisha cried, grabbing Ramon's lifeless hand.

"It's not your fault, Nisha. It was an accident," Vonshee said.

"Yes, it is. I let my emotions get the best of me and now look at him. Look at what we did to him. We shot the father of my unborn. He's hooked to a fucking breathing machine. Why is he even back in Houston?" Nisha asked as she turned to Charles for answers.

Charles looked at Nisha. "I picked him up from the airport this morning. He wanted to visit the new location of the operation. We went to the mansion to change, Ramon decided he wanted to drive his Challenger. We rode around for a little before we seen your car run a red light. He wanted to surprise you. When y'all turned down that street, y'all jumped out and started firing at us. The shit was crazy."

"We didn't know it was y'all. We thought it was J-Dub."

Charles raised his eyebrow. "Why would you be shooting at J-Dub?"

Nisha wiped her eyes. "I set him up to get his location. After we got there, he basically confessed to being a part of my brother's murder. I couldn't control myself and I shot him."

"What?" Charles asked.

"We thought he was following us. We had just left his house."

"Come on, Nisha. Why wouldn't you wait for me and Ramon?"

"Because he fucked with a Pretty Diva," Nisha answered with watered eyes.

Charles stared at her with the look of understanding on his face.

Nisha shook her head. "You know he wanted to be Ramon so bad. He went and bought a car that looks just like his."

"Yeah, I know," Charles responded.

Nisha turned to Ramon and burst out crying. All the of Pretty Divas surrounded her to comfort their leader.

"What am I going to do?" Nisha cried out.

The room fell to a complete silence then it was broken by the ringing of Nisha's phone.

Nisha pulled out her phone and looked at the screen and noticed a very unfamiliar number. She told herself not to answer it, but answered anyway.

"Hello," she answered in a low tone.

"Well, if it isn't the leader of the Bitch Divas," the caller said in a taunting voice.

"Who the fuck is this?" Nisha asked with an attitude.

"Wouldn't you like to know. But I'm pretty sure you already know who this is. Remember July, your grand opening on your birthday. To be honest, I thought it was a beautiful day for a shooting."

"If I know who you are, why would you need a voice changer?" Nisha asked.

"If you really want to know what happened to your brother and if you really want all of this to come to an end, then meet me at the abandoned warehouse on Richmond Avenue and Industrial Road."

"Sounds like a fucking setup," Nisha said.

"1311 Richmond and come alone," the taunting voice said before the phone went silent.

"What the hell?" Nisha said as she stared at her phone.

"Who was it?'" Bree asked.

"Honestly, I don't know. But they told me to come alone. And they said if I wanted this to come to an end to meet them at the abandoned warehouse on Richmond Blvd."

"Aw hell no," Vonshee said. "We're coming with you."

"No," Nisha said.

"We're all Pretty Divas, Nisha. So we're coming with you, *Mami*," Selena said, putting her hand on Nisha's shoulder.

"I think they're serious," Charles said.

"Okay, fine but y'all stay in the car. I'll call if I need y'all," Nisha said, staring at Ramon.

"Fuck no, we'll give you fifteen minutes and if you don't come out, then we're coming in with guns blazing,"

Nisha slightly smiled. "Okay, fine."

"You girls better be strapped. I'll stay with Ramon. I was at the scene so I have to stay here. When the cops get here, I already have a cover story."

THE PRETTY DIVA STORY

"Vonshee, keep me updated on everything," Charles said, eyeing the Divas.

CHAPTER 30 – THE PRETTY SHOWDOWN

Nisha entered the abandoned warehouse filled with emotions. The building was dusty, gloomy and cold. She searched for a light but realized it was a little pointless. Using her phone to give the space more light, she drew her weapon and yelled, "I'm here, now what's the point in calling me out if you're no going to show up?"

"I didn't think you would make it," a voice said.
Nisha looked around until she set her eyes on a man stepping from the shadows.

"Who the fuck are you and what the hell do you want with me?" she asked.

"Oh, do forgive me. Allow me to introduce myself, formally. I'm Detective Black." Black said with a malevolent smile.

"And, that's supposed to mean what to me?" Nisha asked, raising her .380.

"Well, you did shoot my son earlier, didn't you?"

"I don't know what you're talking about."

"I think you do," Black said, raising his Glock.

"I think you know what happened to my brother. We've discovered you were the one who was over his case. You were the first to the scene at a place no one dares to go," Black laughed.

"So, you do know me."

"Does it matter?"

Black grinned. "No it doesn't, because you're going to end up just like your brother for what you did to my son. You fucked him up pretty bad."

"Like I said, I don't know what you're talking about. And, maybe your son deserved whatever happened to him."

"Maybe, " Black laughed, "But like a good father, I'm here to clean up his shit,"

BANG!!

Black fired but missed. Nisha ran and hid behind a pallet of bagged salt rocks. She rose and fired two shots in Black's direction. The bullets whistled and ricocheted off the steal pillars.

"You know you're just like your brother," Black yelled. "You both fail to see things of the future."

Nisha peaked around a pillar. "So, you murdered my brother because he didn't want a future with you and your family?"

Black laughed. "On the contrary, your brother was closer to my family than you think. I could've protected his business, made it bigger, better, and untouchable. See, I'm the King of this City! With my connections and Cory's mind, we could have been unstoppable."

"You're just a dirty cop with an ego problem."

"You know me so well." Black laughed.

"I know people like you," Nisha said, stepping out into a spotlight from an outside source shining through a window.

"Oh, do you now?"

"Yup," Nisha said, raising her gun.

Black stepped out from behind a pile of boxes.

"I know more about you, Nisha. I know you were a bank worker who got bored with life and became a drug dealer. You thought you could become your brother.

You fell in love with Ramon and started that Pretty Diva shit with a group of undeserving gold digging bitches. See, when Cory died, my son and daughter was supposed to take over, Ramon not quitting like he planned fucked that up."

"What do you mean, your daughter?" Nisha yelled, confused.

Black laughed. "Like I said, you're just like your brother. You fail to see the things that's right in front of you."

"We already know about Kareem, who goes by Karmen now. She hasn't spoke to y'all in years. But, what does she have to do with this?" Nisha asked.

"Nothing, but my first born has everything to do with it."

"You're not making any sense, cop."

"Maybe, maybe not," Black said with a slight smirk.

"Why the hell do you have that smirk on your fucking face?"

"Really? I'm surprised you can't put this puzzle together. Let me help, so we can get this over with. Allow me to introduce you to someone you might know very well, my daughter and my oldest, Karla Morgan Black. She goes by Mrs.Boudreaux now."

"What?" Nisha said as Cory's wife walked through a set of double doors. Nisha's emotions went through the roof as Karla chained the door behind her.

"Are you fucking serious?" Nisha asked shocked, recognizing the hoodie Karla was wearing.

"I told Cory to cut my family in and he wouldn't listen to me. My brother would have brought his operation to new heights. With my father's protection, we could have really been on top. But Cory wouldn't have it. He disrespected me and my family and you see where that got him," Karla laughed.

"You little bitch!" Nisha said, turning her gun toward Karla.

"Not so fast," Black said, putting his gun on Nisha.

"You had his kids," Nisha said.

"Really?" Karla asked.

"You think those are his kids? Cory spent so much time growing at those houses, he didn't have no time to give me children."

"You dirty bitch," Nisha screamed as she squeezed the trigger to her gun.

BANG!

A bullet from Nisha's gun pierced through Karla's arm forcing her to drop her .38 Special. Karla dropped to the floor in pain grabbing her shoulder.

"Bitch!" she yelled as Nisha made a dash and ducked behind a stack of boxes.

Detective Black moved in close but Nisha fired to keep him at a distance. She turned to Karla, who was picking up her weapon. Nisha fired shots at the floor causing Karla to jump back. Nisha looked at the exit door to see if she could make a run for it. But the bolted chains made the idea small. Her next thought was to shoot her way out.

A banging on the glass got Nisha's attention. It was the Pretty Divas, unable to enter into the building.

"Come out, come out, come out and play," Black said.

Nisha ducked and maneuvered through the aisle. She saw a shadow run by in front of her, but she couldn't tell who it was. A bullet bounced off of a steel cage as she made her way down the aisle.

"You know, Nisha," Karla's voice echoed.

"You really shouldn't have made your diva bitches wait in the car. Now, they can't save you."

Black laughed. "No one can save her."

"Nisha, Nisha, Nisha. You know I did love your brother once, before he became Mr. Do Goodie," Karla said.

Nisha peaked up and saw Karla creeping by, she pulled her trigger multiple times. Karla ducked and ran behind a pallet of stacked boxes. Nisha snuck around until she reached Kala from behind. Twenty feet away, Nisha squeezed her trigger but her clip was empty. Shocked and mad, she made a quick decision to fight. Nisha charged at Kala from behind and tackled her to the ground. Karla's gun flew out of her hands and landed on the floor as both women hit the pavement.

"Fucking bitch," Nisha yelled as she swung a fist across Karla's face. Karla flipped over and Nisha caught her with another blow. Next, she pulled Karla's hair and threw a fury of punches at Karla's head as she tried to escape the assault.

"Get off me bitch," Karla yelled as she kicked Nisha in the stomach, knocking the wind out of her. The pain sent Nisha to the ground and it reminded her she was four weeks pregnant. Karla took the time to recover then soccer kicked Nisha in the ribs.

Nisha gasped in pain, holding her side, she went down.

"You fight just like your bitch ass brother," Karla said, spitting out blood.

"Fuck you, Karla. You're just another gold digging hoe with daddy issues you Doja Cat looking hoe."

"I resent that remark," Detective Black said, walking up from behind.

Nisha slowly stood, looked at Karla and charged once again, until both ladies slammed into a pile of boxes. Nisha punched and pounded Karla's face with all of her might. "Fuck you, bitch," she yelled as she delivered the blow that knocked Karla out cold.

"Get your ugly pretty diva ass off my daughter," Detective Black said as he put his barrel to Nisha's temple.

Nisha slowly put her hands up and rose to her feet. "Yup, now you want to shoot me because you saw me whip your daughter's ass."

"What can I say, I like to see a clean fight. I raised my children to fight, but to also go down swinging and she did."

"Really?" Nisha asked. "I'm gonna take a wild guess that something must had happened to J-Dub. My brother beat his ass in front of you and you shot him?"

Black laughed. "Damn bitch, you think you're smart ass hell, huh? The funny thing about this is, this is the same gun I shot him with. I got it from this cop. Tell Cory to rot in pieces when you see him. Now-"

BANG, BANG!

Black's talking was cut short, two bullets pierced his flesh. Nisha turned around and watched Black's body hit the ground. Nisha looked up and saw a very familiar face, Simeerah Knowles, her friend from high school and her childhood best friend. Nisha glanced a Karla's gun.

"Don't do it, Nisha," Knowles said, pointing her weapon.

"What are you going to do? Are you going to arrest me?" Nisha asked as she slowly picked up Karla's gun.

"Please," Knowles begged, "Drop it."

"Are you going to arrest me?" Nisha asked again.

"For what?" Knowles asked, approaching her slowly.

"For what I did to J-Dub and Karla."

"As far as I'm concerned, I didn't see anything."

Nisha turned to Karla. "This bitch got my brother killed and had him raising kids that wasn't even his."

"I understand, Nisha. But if you pull that trigger I can not let you walk out of here."

Nisha looked at Karla in disgust, then turned to Knowles. "So, a detective is what you left to become. I would've never guessed. I would have assumed a business owner or something."

"Well, you know life. It sends you in directions that you wouldn't dare to go, Queen Pin."

Nisha dropped the gun and backed away. Knowles ran over to check Detective Black's pulse.

"This bastard right here had a lot of things going on. I've been tracking and following him daily, but I didn't know he was linked to y'all."

Knowles stepped over to Karla and handcuffed her. "You're under arrest for helping and aiding in the murder of Cory Beaudruex."

Nisha watched her long time friend put the cuffs on Karla and site her Miranda Rights. "So, I'm free to go?" she asked.

Knowles stood up straight and stared Nisha down. "You know me and Black had a conversation about doing the right thing when our honor and badge will be put to test."

Nisha watched Knowles fuddle with keys she got out of Karla's pocket. She assumed they were the keys to the locked chain.

"And, what is the right thing to do?" Nisha asked.

Knowles paused. "The right thing to do is to tell you, the rest of the Pretty Divas are waiting for you outside.

Knowles threw Nisha the keys to the lock. "Right thing to do is to let you go?"

"Thank you, Detective," Nisha said in relief.

"You're welcome, Ms. Beaudruex."

Nisha turned around, walked toward the door, and stopped. "You know we really missed you. It was never the same after you left."

Knowles smiled. "I was never the same after I left," she sighed. "You better leave, I have to call in and make something up for this dead officer."

"Maybe not." Nisha reached in her pocket and grabbed a digital voice recorder. "Everything you'll need is on this, I'm sure."

Nisha tossed the digital recorder to Knowles, smiled, and made her way out of the building.

*****

"What the fuck, Nisha?" Bree said as Nisha approached them. "We couldn't get inside, we heard gunshots, and we almost called the cops."

"We need to leave right now because they're on their way," Nisha said.

The Pretty Diva asked no questions as they all entered the vehicle. Nisha started her car and slowly pulled away from the scene. On her way out she spotted a blacked out Chevy Impala with the plates that read, 'PDI-VAS2'.

She smiled. "I think I need to get checked and I want to go see Ramon."

"I think you need to get your brain checked. You've been doing some crazy ass shit lately. We need to lay low for a bit," Vonshee said.

"You're right Vonshee?" Selena said from the backseat. "Nisha, *Que paso, Mami?*"

"English please," Nisha said with a slight painful laugh, holding her stomach turning onto a main street.

"Girl, tell us what happened," Selena responded.

"Okay, okay, I'll tell you on the way to the hospital, we need to get out of this area first. Are y'all coming with me to see Ramon?" Nisha asked.

"Duh." Bree said.

"What kind of question is that?" Vonshee asked. "Of course we're coming with you to see him."

Nisha smiled. "Well good, because it wouldn't be a Pretty Diva story without the man who put everything together."

EPILOGUE

Detective Knowles sat as Chief Taylor closed a folder and tossed it onto her desk. The Mayor was proud of the department for solving three cages at one time. The FBI left after the solving of the cases and Knowles was proud of herself for doing such a great job. Everyone pressed Knowles about the mystery voice recorder and its origin, but she never told a soul.

"How was your night, Chief?" Knowles asked, taking a seat.

"It could have been better," the Chief said, sipping her coffee. "Lopez Informed me that you wanted some time off. A vacation?"

"Yeah, I just want and need a little break, I need to hit a reset button."

Maybe just a week or two."

"Understood, and fantastic work out there, but next time take your partner and that's a direct order."

Knowles shook her head, "So, what's the update on Karla Beaudruex?"

"Mrs. Beaudruex will get what's coming to her."

"Chief, it was never my intention to take out Detective Black, he just got caught in the middle of everything. I didn't even know he was involved,"

"It's totally understandable, Knowles."

"Are you sure?" Knowles asked.

"Yes, sometimes these things happen. So, go home, take some time off, get some rest and don't stress about anything. You had a hunch and you went with it and it helped solve three cases."

"Thanks, Chief," Knowles said with a smile.

Detective Knowles left the Chief's office and was stopped by her partner. "When can we expect you back?" Lopez asked.

"In a couple of weeks," Knowles responded, giving Lopez a hug.

"Good, call me later."

"I will."

"You better," Lopez said with a laugh.

Knowles smiled, turned on her heels and headed out of the Hall.

"Wait," Lopez said, stopping Knowles one last thing before you go. "You care to do lunch with me?"

"I would partner, but have an appointment at The Pretty Diva's Hair Salon and Nails."

"Get it then, girl," Lopez said, snapping her fingers in the air twice.

"You know it, "Knowles laughed, cat walking out of the office.

Knowles pulled out her phone and dialed Fantasia's personal number.

"Hello," Fantasia answered.

Knowles laughed. "Hey, Fanny. I'm on my way."

*****

The Chief re-opened the folder she threw on her desk. She glanced at Knowles walking out of the office, then she turned to the photos in front of her. She never thought she would see Detective Black dead. How could she? He was the love of her life at one point in time. Yes, he left her for someone younger and more beautiful but she still loved him. She flipped to the next page and stared at the photos of Nisha, Vonshee, Bree, Fantasia and Selena.

The Chief's personal phone rang, snapping her from her revengeful thoughts. "Chief Taylor," she answered.

"Really, Mom?"

"Well, I'm at work. What did you expect, Jeremy?"

"I just left from visiting Karla."

"And, you're telling me this because?"

J-Dub laughed. "Well, let's just say I know a way to bring them Pretty Diva bitches down."

"How?" the Chief asked, sipping her coffee again.

"First things first. We need to stage another fire."

The Pretty Diva Story
2
The Pretty Saga Continues

COMING SOON

ABOUT THE AUTHOR

Rocko "Main1" Dupas is from Houston, Texas. He is also a Father, Author, Musician, and the owner of Corporate G'z Entertainment. He's also a self taught sound engineer that's has always had a love for writing. Currently, Mr. Dupas is working on his next 2 projects. The Pretty Diva Story 2 and Xesia : The Reawakening, an urban horror story.

Contact and reviews

www.facebook.com/Rocko Dupas

www.Instagram.com/Rocko_on_tha_keyz

Made in the USA
Columbia, SC
04 February 2023

11232253R00137